P9-CLE-912

The
Penny
Whistle

The Penny Whistle

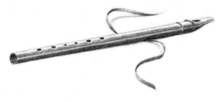

B.J. Hoff

BETHANY HOUSE PUBLISHERS
MINNEAPOLIS, MINNESOTA 55438

Published by Bethany House Publishers
A Ministry of Bethany Fellowship, Inc.
11300 Hampshire Avenue South
Minneapolis, Minnesota 55438

Printed in the United States of America.

ISBN 1–55661–877–8

"The Lord is my strength and my song."
–Exodus 15:2 NIV

The Penny Whistle

Northeastern Kentucky, 1890s

Maggie MacAuley could pinpoint the exact day when the music stopped in Skingle Creek. It was the same day some no-account unknown stole Mister Stuart's silver flute. The same day Mister Stuart seemed to give up and began to change.

The only schoolteacher who had ever stayed for more than a few months, Mister Stuart had arrived fresh from the state university almost five years ago. He never talked much about himself, only that he had grown up in Lexington. How or why he had ended up in a little mining town like Skingle Creek was anyone's guess, but to everyone's surprise, he had settled right in and stayed put.

Maggie had been only six when Mister Stuart came to town, but she could still recollect his first day at the school. For weeks after his arrival, the townsfolk had gone on about how "that new teacher, he sure is a different sort."

The older students, like Maggie's sisters Eva Grace and Nell Frances, claimed to have known right from the start that their new teacher was indeed a "different sort." If truth were told, not a soul in Skingle Creek—child or grown-up—had ever seen the likes of a man like Jonathan Stuart.

Maggie figured Mister Stuart must be what was meant by a "gentle man." His smile was gentle; his speech was gentle—even his walk was quiet and easy-like. He had a way of making it seem that whatever he happened to be doing at the moment was the most important thing he had to do all day—and that the students in their one-room schoolhouse were the most important people in the world.

Mister Stuart never seemed to be in a hurry or lose his patience or raise his voice. Although he had himself a fine gold watch, he seldom took it out of his vest pocket, except when it came time to change from one class to another or to ring the dismissal bell.

Even when Lester Monk—who everyone knew was the slowest one boy to ever put shoes on in the morning—lumbered through his sums or went to stuttering when he tried to read more than two or three words in a row, Mister Stuart would just smile and nod, as if to encourage Lester to keep on trying, they had all the time in the world.

Maggie was pretty sure that any other teacher would have bawled Lester out something fierce or maybe even smacked his hand with the yardstick and made him stand in the dumb-corner. But not Mister Stuart. He treated all his students the same, even Lester.

Another thing that was different about their teacher was the way he had of almost always making A POINT. Mister Stuart, he was a great one for making A POINT.

His stories, for example, always had A POINT to them. He told the best stories of anyone in Skingle Creek—even better than

Maggie's uncle Ruff, whose tall tales were known throughout the county. Mister Stuart's stories were always crammed with enough excitement to make a body's heart hammer and enough adventure to satisfy even the older boys in the classroom. Sometimes he told them stories from the Holy Bible. He never had to read the stories from the Bible, for he seemed to know each one by heart. Sometimes he told them stories about animals or people who had lived long ago. "Folk tales," he called them.

But no matter what kind of story he told, there was usually A POINT, though Mister Stuart didn't always come right out and *say* what the point *was*. You just knew, by the way he would end the story and stand there, watching the class with a little smile, that the story had contained A POINT, and he was hoping they had caught on to it.

Many of Mister Stuart's stories had to do with God and how He loved people and all the creatures He had made—even toads and spiders, which Maggie thought must take a *lot* of love. Mister Stuart said that nothing was ever hopeless with God, because He could change anything, including people.

Oftentimes, Mister Stuart's stories seemed to have A POINT about being kind to others, even to those who weren't kind to *you*, or about the harm that gossip could cause, or how it was wrong to be envious of folks who seemed to have more money and possessions than *you* did.

That particular point wasn't much of a problem in Skingle Creek. Except for Dr. Woodbridge and Judson Tallman, the mine manager, everyone in town was fixed about the same when it came to money: no one had any.

Skingle Creek was a company town where everyone took their living from the coal mines. According to Maggie's mother, it wasn't much of a living. Mum said that what the company store didn't get on pay-day, the tavern did.

That's why she and Maggie's father often seemed to be at each other, arguing. Mum would try to make Da turn over his wages before he took off for the tavern, and Da would call her a terrible scold and say how any man who worked twelve hours a day under the ground ought to be able to lift a glass or two on payday if he felt so inclined. It was his way, he would declare with a terrible scowl, of washing the coal dust from his soul.

Maggie thought she understood what he meant. Hadn't she felt the same those times when Mister Stuart played his silver flute? Somehow the music had seemed to wash the coal dust and all the other dingy thoughts and feelings right out of her soul.

The music was a glory, a wondrous thing entirely. Sometimes it was like a graceful bird, winging up and over the clouds. Other times, it was more like shiny coins tumbling out of an angel's knapsack. And sometimes—and to Maggie these were the best times of all—it was like a happy waterfall, pouring down from heaven itself over the town, washing away the ugly black dust that coated the unpainted company houses and the laundry on the clotheslines—and even a body's hair.

During these special times, Maggie could almost pretend the whole town and even life itself had been washed clean and

made new by the music from Mister Stuart's silver flute. But now the flute was gone, stolen by somebody who either didn't know how important it was ... or didn't care.

Meanwhile, from the looks of him, Mister Stuart was getting sicker and weaker by the day. Of late, he seemed to scarcely have the strength to write their assignments on the blackboard.

Mum had always claimed that Mister Stuart was "sickly." Some of the other grownups had also remarked how the teacher just kept getting "poorer and poorer," that there "wasn't enough of him to stand against a strong wind."

It shamed Maggie to admit it, but up until recently, she and the other students hadn't paid all that much attention to their teacher's poor health. Mister Stuart had always been a lean man—thinner than most, she reckoned—but almost everyone in Skingle Creek was on the lean side. Other than the Woodbridges and the Tallmans, no one in town got enough to eat to make them fleshy.

But even though she couldn't actually point to the exact day when Mister Stuart's health had taken a turn for the worse, Maggie *could* recall when the light had seemed to go out of him; when he had stopped smiling as he once had and no longer hummed or whistled softly to himself; and when, instead of walking up and down the aisles to help them with their papers, he had taken to sitting at his desk most of the day. He had even stopped telling his stories with A POINT. Most of the time now he simply assigned the class a number of pages to read on their own.

The fact was that since the morning he had discovered his silver flute missing, Mister Stuart hadn't been the same. And neither had anything else.

––––––––––

Jonathan Stuart watched the faces of the children as they filed into the classroom and slid behind their desks.

He always thought of them as *his* children, as if they were a special gift entrusted to him by God—albeit an almost frightening responsibility. As his gaze came to rest on first one, then another, he couldn't quell the bitter question that had nagged at him for days now: *who among them could have done such a thing?*

And *why?*

Although he found it unthinkable that any one of his students might have had so little regard for him—or for something that belonged to him—he realized that in all likelihood the one responsible for the theft of the flute was right here, in this classroom.

He watched Kenneth Tallman take his seat and discounted him almost immediately. The narrow, bespectacled face was that of an unhappy child who, in spite of belonging to one of the few financially comfortable households in town, never seemed quite at ease with the other students—or with himself, for that matter.

The boy glanced up, giving the uncertain smile that never failed to touch Jonathan's heart. No, not only did this reticent youth have no reason to steal from his teacher, but of all the children in the room, he was probably one of only two or three who wouldn't have had the daring to attempt such an exploit.

Lester Monk now trudged up the aisle. He stumbled—a common occurrence with Lester—but gave Jonathan a self-disparaging grin as he righted himself and slid behind his desk. Jonathan smiled back, studying the boy. Certainly Lester's family could use the money an underhanded sale of the flute might bring. But somehow Jonathan couldn't see the plodding, slow-witted Lester as the culprit. The youth simply didn't have the imagination to concoct such a scheme, much less the mental agility to carry it off. Lester was clumsy, often inept, but he was no thief. Of that, Jonathan was confident.

Behind Lester came Maggie MacAuley and little Summer Rankin, great friends who, admittedly, were two of Jonathan's favorite students. Even though he had always tried to discipline himself against the folly of having favorites in the classroom, it was hard not to be partial to these two, different though they were in age and temperament.

Maggie MacAuley, with her riot of fiery hair and pointed little chin, was probably the brightest child in the one-room schoolhouse. The girl was unfailingly cheerful—her quick, eager smile would have melted the ice under Dunbar's mill in mid-January. She also had a keen wit, an insatiable curiosity, and a hunger to learn that challenged even Jonathan's love of teaching. Maggie's immigrant family was as poor as any in town, but she and her two older sisters were invariably dressed in clean feedsack pinafores, and the parts in their hair appeared to have been cut with a straightedge. Maggie MacAuley had a large heart, an incredible measure of common sense, and seemed to thrive on looking after the younger children in the classroom. She was also, Jonathan had long sensed, a born leader.

No, it simply could not be Maggie.

As for poor little Summer Rankin, Jonathan's heart ached for the child, whose frailty became even more stark when reflected in the glow of Maggie's vibrancy. It would be absurd, and somehow obscene, to consider her even remotely capable of wrongdoing.

Summer was a mere wisp of a child—a tiny, fragile creature whose white-blond hair and pale skin would have given her an almost spectral appearance had it not been for the angry flush of fever that more often than not blotched her hollowed cheeks. Jonathan had it from Dr. Woodbridge himself that the child was consumptive. Of late, she was out of school more than she was in, and even on the days she was present, she sometimes had a distracted, faraway glaze to the eye that made Jonathan wonder just how aware the girl actually was of her surroundings.

Nine-year-old Summer lived on a hill above town in a roughhewn cabin that fairly bulged with people—children and adults. Jonathan had come away from his first visit to the Rankins years ago feeling somewhat dazed by the number of family members who seemed to inhabit that cramped, noisy place. Aging grandparents, aunts and uncles, and no less than six children under the age of twelve had been in evidence the night of his visit. It had struck him as truly remarkable that a delicate, dreamy child like Summer could exist in such shabby bedlam.

For a time, until he had come to know both children better, Jonathan had puzzled over the bond between Maggie MacAuley and Summer Rankin. Eleven-year-old Maggie seemed as strong and self-assured as Summer was frail and shy. While Maggie preferred rousing stories of adventure and sensible, precise lesson assignments, Summer seemed enlivened only by paintings and poetry and music. In fact, this fey child was the only one of his students Jonathan had ever allowed to touch his silver flute. She had shyly asked him once if she might attempt to play, and after only the slightest hesitation, Jonathan had shown her the bare rudiments of technique. To his amazement, within minutes Summer had managed to evoke a simple but plaintive folk melody.

Of course, it had been months now since the girl had had either the breath or the energy to play. Indeed, Jonathan suspected that these days most of Summer's strength had to be conserved for the mere effort of existence.

He watched the two girls take their seats behind their desks, his throat tightening. Maggie was fiercely protective of her ill friend. Even those inclined to bully the younger children seemed reluctant to incur Maggie MacAuley's wrath by tormenting little Summer. With a heavy heart, Jonathan questioned just how much longer Summer Rankin would be around for Maggie to protect. He could almost see the girl failing. He wondered if Maggie saw it, too, and rather hoped she did. Otherwise, it would only go harder for her when she had to face the truth.

One after another, the children slipped into their seats, Jonathan dismissing each as a potential thief with little more than a glance. They were better than that, a part of him insisted. Surely none was capable of such cruelty. For he could not shake the thought that, even though the flute *might* have been stolen for its monetary value, it could just as likely have been taken as a way of delivering a personal wound to *him*.

In that event, the offender must be someone with a grudge against him, or, at the very least, someone who disliked him intensely. Was it possible that one of the children—*his* children—could actually bear such animosity toward him without his knowing?

While the possibility appalled him, Jonathan was not altogether ignorant of the human nature's capacity for meanness or duplicity. His years of association with children and their families had introduced him to a dismaying mélange of cruelties of which both the young and their elders are capable. He had, therefore, long ago lost his youthful naïveté and most of his earlier faith in the innate goodness of man.

Yet, with all their faults, these children were like family to him. Indeed, he loved them almost as much as if they *were* his family—perhaps because their *need* to be loved was so great. It hadn't taken Jonathan long to realize that the children of Skingle Creek had known little in the way of love or gentleness or any real beauty in their young lives. This dark cavern of a town, carved from the bottom side of a mountain, seemed to exist in the shadows. If the coal dust from the mines hadn't smudged the face of the entire town, the lowering gloom from the surrounding hills would have. It was a gray, hopeless place in which to live, and sooner or later, most of those within its confines became a gray, hopeless people.

Survival seemed the town residents' only achievement, their only success. Many were uneducated, even illiterate. The men broke their backs and destroyed their lungs by hammering and picking away at the bowels of the earth. Most of them never saw daylight; they went belowground before daybreak and emerged, half-blind and hunched like gnomes, well after sundown.

The miners and their families seemed to live bitter, joyless lives from which escape was virtually impossible. It hadn't taken Jonathan long to learn that the mining company had structured a brilliantly ruth-less system that worked altogether to the company's advantage. It was a system that bordered on enslavement. The company owned the store that represented the min-ers' only source of food and clothing. The company also provided the only "clinic" where medical treatment could be obtained. They even let the building that presently housed the school.

The truth was that the company owned the town and, for all intents and purposes, the miners themselves.

Jonathan Stuart had come to Skingle Creek with the somewhat quixotic intention of paying a debt. His family in Lexington, prosperous and endowed with a rare social conscience, had impressed upon him throughout his adolescent years that wealth entailed Christian responsibility rather than

worldly privilege. Upon graduation from college, Jonathan had taken the position as schoolmaster here in Skingle Creek thinking to satisfy that responsibility, even seeing it as "a call" to teach and nurture the underprivileged. He had come to the grim little mining town as an idealistic if well-intentioned youth, but one who had known little about human nature and even less about children.

While he had learned more than he cared to know about people in general over the years, he was determined to give those under his care what they seemed to need more than anything else—more than whatever knowledge or skills or even affection he could offer them. He was determined to give them the gift of *hope*.

At some point, Jonathan had committed himself to helping his children to see their town, the world beyond—and, yes, even life itself—through eyes of hope. From that time on, inasmuch as he was able, he attempted to introduce them to things of truth and beauty and goodness—those things he believed to be bestowed by a loving Creator upon His beloved creation, things that, once planted, would ultimately give bloom to the gift of hope.

Jonathan's tenure at Skingle Creek had changed his life, broadening and testing his faith, challenging him in a variety of ways as a man and as a teacher. At the same time, he had been drawn into the town, made a part of the children's world and the lives of their families as well.

For a long time, his busy, fulfilling life had made it possible, almost easy, to ignore the increasing symptoms of a heart ailment that had actually begun in his childhood. Most of the time, he managed to disregard the shortness of breath, the increasing weakness and chronic fatigue. Once he had actually traveled back to Lexington to see a specialist. The diagnosis had only made him that much more determined to delay, if not defy, the inevitable. The children needed him, he would remind himself when the weariness grew almost debilitating. *The children were depending on him* became his own clarion call to arms when the tide of battle with the relentless illness seemed to turn against him.

Always, there were the children.

But lately he had begun to wonder if he hadn't finally lost the battle. He felt old—decades older than his years—old, and used, and so very, very tired. Was it merely coincidence that something deep inside his spirit seemed to have abandoned him with the theft of the flute? It was as if the sun had finally gone down on his own soul and left him cold and barren: without light, without music, and without hope.

His parents had given him the silver flute when he was still a boy, after much cajoling on his part. Even then, without knowing *how* he knew, he had somehow recognized the stirring of music within himself as something vital, something God-given, as essential to his life as air or water.

From the first, with only a minimum of instruction, the music that had poured forth from the flute had been pure joy—an exultation—and at the same time, a balm of healing. It was almost as if the music had been inside him forever, merely waiting for an instrument to set it free and give it life.

And once loosed, it seemed to bring a touch of something beyond the normal, the commonplace, to everything within its reach.

Jonathan had seen a similar response in his students. It appeared that the music lifted them beyond the grim reality of their surroundings and let them catch a glimpse of goodness and beauty, of hope and heavenly things. For Jonathan's part, when he played the flute for the children, he felt a oneness—a bond—with them and with his God that he felt at no other time.

Most astonishing of all, he actually felt *strong*—energized and renewed, as though the illness and the wasting of his heart had been only a dream or a vague memory. The pain and exhaustion seemed to fall away. So exhilarated, so exultant did he become that he felt his body could scarcely contain his jubilant spirit.

But no longer. For days now he had found himself giving in to the pain, to the weakness and the exhaustion. His spirit felt leaden, as cold as he imagined the underground mine shafts must feel in the dead of winter, and just as dark.

Whether it was his inability to accept

the possible deceit of one of his children, or whether it was simply God's way of telling him that his job here was done, his resolve to live to the fullest, to make every last moment of his life count, had little by little given way to a kind of bleak resignation, a numbing sense of defeat.

If it sometimes occurred to him that his behavior was bizarre, even irrational—the mere theft of a piece of crafted silver should not bring a man to such despair, after all—Jonathan suppressed the thought, telling himself that of course it was far more complicated than that. The loss of the instrument was only a part of his desolation, although he was aware, at times uncomfortably so, that he somehow found the act symbolic—as if the theft of the flute might herald something even worse.

In any event, he sensed the need to accept the fact that he was seriously and incurably ill. The end of his life, he had begun to speculate, might very well be imminent.

The possibility that he might soon have to leave the community and the people he had come to love, especially the children, brought him an almost unbearable sense of grief. Yet, as the days went on and he grew more weary, the prospect of death seemed less grim. In most ways, he felt ready to meet his Lord. Although his failures, he was sure, far exceeded his victories, he had tried to live a life pleasing to God, had tried to give more than he had taken from the world. No, he was not afraid of death; on the contrary, these days he thought he would almost welcome it when it came.

Nevertheless, a feeling of restlessness sometimes overcame him, a gnawing sense of something left undone. It came unbidden, at unexpected moments, this irksome prodding at the fringes of his mind. Like an insect that refused to be shaken, the nagging feeling of incompleteness continued to plague him, invading his thoughts, stealing his peace.

Yet, try as he would, he simply could not identify the source of his discontent, could not think of any reason to struggle on. In fact, it seemed to Jonathan Stuart that all that was left to him now was to accept the inevitable ... and wait to die.

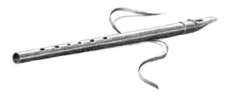

Almost a month after the silver flute turned up missing, Maggie MacAuley decided that something must be done about Mister Stuart. He looked to be growing thinner and thinner, and when Lily Woodbridge had made mention of the fact only the day before that the teacher looked *faded*, Maggie had seen at a glance what she meant. Mister Stuart was beginning to remind her of her mother's good Sunday tablecloth. At one time the cloth had been bright and colorful, with golden loaves of bread and blue milk jugs painted on it, but it was now faded from so many launderings it had hardly any color left to it.

Sometimes Maggie would find herself gripped by the dread thought that one day their teacher, too, would simply fade away to nothing. They would look up from their books ... and Mister Stuart would be gone.

He was terrible quiet these days—so quiet that sometimes they almost forgot he was even in the schoolroom. He was still thorough with the lessons and gave them proper instruction, but more and more often now, he allowed them to work by themselves rather than taking part in what he called "class discussions."

Truth be told, Mister Stuart didn't even seem to notice when the pesky Crawford twins acted up. If they got too rambunctious, he would just look at them with his sad, tired eyes, and pretty soon Dinah and Duril would cease their mischief, as if they knew their teacher didn't have the strength to discipline them.

Maggie was determined to do something to help Mister Stuart, and the sooner the better. Today, because it had been snowing on and off most of the morning, she and the other children had stayed inside to eat their lunches. But early in the afternoon the sky had cleared, and Mister Stuart had sent them outside to take some fresh air. Now everyone was standing around the school yard, their breath spiraling up in little smokestacks, combining to form a cloud over their heads.

"We have to help Mister Stuart," Maggie said, looking from one to the other for confirmation.

Summer Rankin bobbed her head up and down, sending her fair hair into a puff of a halo about her face. "Mister Stuart is bad sick," she said. She started to add something more, but instead broke into a fit of coughing. These days, Summer was nearly always coughing.

"His *heart* is sick," said Lily Woodbridge, her face pinched in a wise-old-owl expression. "My daddy said so." As the daughter of Skingle Creek's only doctor, Lily offered every comment as though the entire town had been holding its breath, waiting to hear from her.

Maggie had heard *her* da say that Lebreen Woodbridge was a quack and probably ought not even be doctoring pigs and horses, but Lily took on as though the man made house calls on the governor himself.

Never one to tolerate Lily's airs, Maggie offered her own observation on Mister Stuart's state of health. "His heart is *broken*," she said, ignoring Lily's sour look. "He's that sad because he doesn't have his flute anymore. The music has gone out of him."

Junior Tyree, the son of the town junkman, dug the toe of his shoe at a rock embedded in the ground. Junior's people were the only Negroes in Skingle Creek, and as a rule he didn't have much to say about anything that went on, which was just as well, since folks probably wouldn't have paid him any mind. To Maggie's way of thinking, though, Junior had more sense than lots of white people she knew, and she for one had learned to pay attention when he volunteered an opinion.

"He's gonna leave," said Junior, studying his foot as he went on scuffing his toe on the rock. "Mister Stuart won't be staying around much longer. He thinks one of us took his flute."

Maggie was close to taking back her opinion of Junior's good sense. "Don't talk crazy, Junior Tyree," she warned. "Mister Stuart wouldn't think any such thing. He knows us better than that."

Junior looked up, his round chocolate eyes squinting at Maggie. Junior always squinted, for though he could scarcely see the tip of his own nose, he was too poor for spectacles. Of them all, only Kenny Tallman could afford to wear eyeglasses. "How you figure?" said Junior. "Who else is he gonna think did it 'sides one of us?"

His statement brought on an angry buzz from the others. "You better just hush, Junior Tyree!" Lily Woodbridge pushed up to Junior, her hands on her hips, her blond sausage curls wagging. "You don't know anything!" Her eyes narrowed. "Or maybe you *do*. Maybe it was *you* who stole Mister Stuart's flute, and that's why you're so sure he suspects one of us."

"Oh, be quiet, Lily," Maggie muttered. Junior might have said a dumb thing, but he wouldn't have stolen Mister Stuart's flute, and Lily knew that just as well as the next. Junior was just like his daddy, Amos, and didn't her da always remark that you could take Amos Tyree's word to the bank, he was that honest? "It seems to me that what we need to be doing is working out a plan to help Mister Stuart instead of standing here quarreling at one another."

She looked at the others—first Summer, then Lily and Lester and Kenny. The problem was too big for the lot of them. But her mother always maintained that you had to start where you were or you'd never get anywhere at all. That being the case, Maggie took a deep breath and proceeded to speak her mind.

"I been thinking," she said, waiting until the others quieted before going on. "Now we can all of us see that Mister Stuart is just getting weaker and more sorrowful since his flute was stolen. That's what got him to feeling so poorly in the first place, I expect. He's always been a little peaked, but when the flute got stolen, it made him worse. He might have been all right, had we been able to find the flute."

"But we *didn't* find it," Kenny Tallman

pointed out, as if Maggie needed to be reminded. He pushed his eyeglasses up a little higher on the bridge of his nose. "And we must have looked everywhere. We only gave up because we ran out of places to search."

Kenny was right, but Maggie didn't much like hearing it. "Well, then," she said, "the only thing we can do is to replace the flute. Now, Mister Stuart's birthday is coming up—it's December 22, remember—almost Christmas. So I was thinking that somehow we might give him a birthday gift *and* a Christmas gift—" She paused, then added, drawing out the words for emphasis, "a ... brand ... new ... flute."

She might just as well have announced that they were going to blow up Bread Loaf Mountain with a firecracker. The lot of them stared at her as if she had lost her wits entirely. But Maggie pressed ahead before they could launch into an argument. "Losing the flute has got a lot to do with Mister Stuart's misery, don't you see? Isn't he always talking about how important music is? Remember last spring, when we were practicing the songs for the Easter program, how he said he wouldn't even like to think about life without music?"

Some of them nodded. "He said he reckoned music is to the soul like food is to the body," Kenny Tallman added. "At least, that's how it seemed to him, he said."

"I recollect best what he told us that one time," Summer Rankin ventured timidly, "about music being 'the voice of the human heart.'"

"And *love* being music to *God's* heart," Maggie put in, newly aware of how truly dreadful Mister Stuart must feel about the loss of his flute.

The others nodded, and she could tell that they, too, were feeling sad for their teacher.

Junior Tyree spoke up again, "Mister Stuart, he said he figured music was p'ert near in-inde*pen*sable."

"Indi*spen*sable," Kenny corrected him promptly.

They were quiet for a time, thinking their own thoughts.

"A silver flute must cost an awful lot of money," Summer said, breaking the silence.

She coughed again, harder this time, and Maggie hunched her own shoulders against the painful sound. These days when Summer coughed, it sounded like crockery breaking somewhere deep down inside of her.

"How much you figure?" asked Junior Tyree.

Summer shrugged, her hand still covering her mouth as the cough subsided.

"A *fortune*, I bet," Lily declared with a dramatic roll of her eyes. "Probably thousands of dollars."

"Maybe not *thousands*"—Kenny Tallman frowned behind his thick spectacles—"but a lot."

"How much is a lot?" Maggie asked, interested only in facts, not guesswork.

Kenny twisted his mouth to one side, thinking. Maggie knew she could depend on his answer. Kenny might be peculiar-like—kind of nervous and fidgety most of the time—but Kenny was smart, all the same. Real smart, especially when it came to money. Maybe because Kenny Tallman was one of the few kids in town who had ever seen much of it, except for the hoity-toity Lily, of course.

"At least *one* thousand dollars," Lily said, revising her earlier estimate before Kenny could reply.

Kenny looked at her. "What do you know about the price of flutes?"

"I *knowwww*," Lily drawled, propping her hands on her hips and eyeballing Kenny like he'd better not question her again.

Kenny just shook his head, as if to say that Lily was minus some buttons. "Maybe not a thousand," he told Maggie, "but a few hundred, at least."

"Might just as *well* be a thousand," Junior Tyree muttered, "for all the chance we got of coming up with that kind of money."

Maggie pulled a face at them all. "Well, it seems to me the thing to do is find out exactly how much we *can* come up with. Kenny, you and Lily and Junior go talk to the kids over by the pump." Maggie wasn't about to approach the older crowd. Her sisters, Nell Frances and Eva Grace, were always hanging out with them, and lately they thought they were too smart to even tell Maggie the time of day. "Me and Summer—Summer and *I*—will ask the others."

She stopped, remembering Lester Monk, who hadn't said a word but was obviously expecting to be included. "Lester, you go with us. We'll ask the Crawfords and Sammy Ray Boyle how much they can give."

"The Crawfords ain't going to have nothing to give," Junior said. "They don't even bring their lunch pails, since their daddy broke his leg in the mine."

Maggie had forgotten about the Crawford twins' bad luck, not that she had much sympathy to spend on *those* two. Duril and Dinah Crawford were just about the biggest bullies in school. Duril could be as mean as a snake sometimes, and Dinah wasn't much better. Still, they were Mister Stuart's students, too.

"Well, ask them anyway," she said. "We need to ask *everyone*. Lester, go find us a jar. There ought to be one in the supply pantry—on the shelf with the paper and paints."

Lester grinned big, as if pleased to be useful, then quickly sobered. "What if Mister Stuart sees me?"

Maggie waved a hand. "Just tell him we need it for outside. He won't ask what it's for."

He turned to go, but Maggie stopped him. "And, Lester," she said, "get a *big* jar, you hear?"

"I'll ask my parents to help," Lily volunteered as Lester took off at a run. "I'm sure they'll want to *contribute*."

Maggie looked at Summer and rolled her eyes at Lily's big word, but she held her tongue. Kenny Tallman said nothing, but nodded in a way that told Maggie he would ask his daddy for help, too. Kenny didn't have a mother; rumor was she had run off with a fiddler from Franklin County a few years back. Judson Tallman, Kenny's daddy, was known to be a hard man and was almost never seen in the company of his son. But maybe Kenny would be able to soften him up, at least for the collection.

Soon everyone was nodding in unspoken understanding that they would approach their parents for a donation.

Silently, Maggie began to tick off the possibilities if all the grown-ups put in money, and her spirits brightened considerably. Not that she or any of the others could expect much from home, of course. Only Kenny and Lily had parents who could afford to part with their money. But she was almost certain that her older sisters would give something from their egg fund, and maybe she could even convince her da to put in a little.

As for herself, she had saved almost five dollars from cleaning the Carlee sisters' house every other Saturday over the past few months. She tried not to think about the fact that she had been saving her wages to buy Christmas presents.

But she had already bought Summer's gift—a scarlet hair ribbon for her "angel hair." Maggie could hand-make her other gifts as she had in the past. A new flute for Mister Stuart was more important than store-bought Christmas presents.

Every little bit would help, and if everyone chipped in *something*—why, there was no telling how much they might end up with.

———————

Their first attempt at a collection was a big disappointment. Scarcely anyone had any money, it seemed, except for Lily Woodbridge and Kenny Tallman. Lily, of course, made a great show of unknotting her handkerchief and putting in "what little she happened to have on her"—which turned out to be only ten cents! Kenny, though, had seventy-five cents, of which he kept only fifteen and put the rest in the jar, promising to bring more the next day.

The older students hadn't been much more help than the younger ones, but at least everyone had put in a little something. Everyone except for the Crawford twins, that is, who claimed the collection was a dumb idea and refused to give a cent. Even knowing that Junior was probably right—that the Crawfords had nothing to give— Maggie thought the least they could have done was keep their hateful remarks to themselves.

She consoled herself with the thought that tomorrow was another day. Almost everyone had agreed to go home and ask their parents for help, so by tomorrow there ought to be more money for the jar.

"That's what we'll *all* do," Lily Woodbridge announced right after school let out. "As soon as we get home, we can ask our parents to *contribute. Some* of us," she said, with deliberate emphasis, "should be able to bring in a lot more tomorrow." The look she angled at Maggie seemed to imply that this would almost certainly not be the case with the mine kids.

Maggie squirmed a little, acknowledg-

ing to herself that Lily was probably right.
Da had all he could do—and didn't he
remind them of it often enough?—just to
keep food on the table for them all. Maggie
was pretty sure she knew how he would
react to the idea of putting money in a jar
for a *musical instrument*.

Still, she had to ask. Everyone else was
going to, so she must do her part. But after
she said good-bye to Summer at the foot of
the hill and turned toward home, she began
to pray in a mighty way that she wouldn't
be the only one besides the Crawford twins
whose folks didn't *contribute*. Especially since
this whole idea had been her doing, after all.

Maggie watched her da closely when he
first arrived home, his face black with coal
dust from the day's work. He was weary as
always, but did not seem overly cross. Even
so, she decided to keep her silence until he
came inside from the washhouse, scrubbed
and wearing his after-work overalls. Still she
delayed, knowing that his mood always
improved some after he ate; she would wait

until he had had his supper.

She helped to clear the table without being asked, then sat squirming with barely controlled impatience while he drank the last of his coffee. Finally, she could wait no longer. She wiped her hands down the sides of her skirt and cleared her throat, allowing the question to come spilling out in a rush, like marbles shaken from a sack. "Da? I was wanting to ask—Mister Stuart's students are taking up a collection, you see, to buy a new flute to replace the one that was stolen, and we agreed to ask all the parents to help. Do you think you could give a bit?"

He turned such a long, silent look on her that Maggie held her breath. At the same time, she was aware of her mother's troubled gaze.

"A *collection*, is it?" Da finally choked out, his face pinched in a terrible scowl.

Maggie managed to nod.

He continued to stare at her. "Are you daft entirely, girl? When it's all I can do to feed the lot of you, you come asking for money for foolishness?"

"Oh, but it's not foolishness at all, Da!"

Maggie blurted out. "Mister Stuart is sick and getting sicker since his silver flute was stolen. We only want to help, don't you see? We only mean to give him back his music."

"What I *see*," her da growled, "is that your Mister Stuart has apparently taught you nothing at all in the way of common sense!"

Maggie was not exactly afraid of her da. He seldom spanked, and when he did, he wasn't as fierce as he let on. But he was a big man, and with his unruly red hair, fiery beard, and flashing green eyes, he could appear terrible mean when he was in a temper. Yet Maggie found his anger less threatening than his contempt. At the moment he was looking at her as if he might be raising himself a fool, and Maggie had all she could do to hold back the scalding tears welling up in her eyes.

She glanced at Eva Grace, then at Nell Frances for some sign of support, but neither would meet her gaze. They sat like two lumps, staring down at their hands as if they had suddenly taken to growing claws.

"Please, Da, would you just let me tell

you?" Maggie ventured again, trying to ignore the tremor in her voice. "Everyone has pledged to bring what they can from home. I'll be putting in my cleaning wages, and Nell Frances and Eva Grace agreed to give some of their egg money, but the only way we can hope to raise enough is if the parents give, too."

She had her sisters' attention now, all right, could feel the two of them glaring at her, while Mum, who had earlier been bouncing Baby Ray on her knee, had gone still as a stone.

Da looked from Maggie to her sisters, his big fists knotted on the table in front of him. "Now you listen to me, you girls, and you listen good. This family has no money to give away." He leaned forward, his eyes hard, his skin flushed—a sure sign that he was holding his temper only with extreme effort. "We all work at this house, except for Baby Ray, whose turn will come soon enough. We work to keep a roof over our heads and clothes on our back and food in the pantry. I expect if one of our neighbors was hungry, we would give him some bread to keep him from starving, but should I *ever* learn that any one of you has wasted hard-earned money on such silliness as you've spoken tonight, you'll sore regret it, you will. I don't go breaking my back from dawn to dark so my children can *throw money away*!"

Maggie could scarcely speak for biting her lip, but she had resolved to risk his wrath in one last attempt. "But, Da, it *wouldn't* be throwing money away! This is *important*! It's for Mister Stuart!"

He banged one fist on the table and shot to his feet, sending the chair flying back against the wall. They all jumped, and Baby Ray began to whimper.

"I'll see Margaret Ann by herself now!" he told them, his tone cutting like a scythe.

Maggie shrank inside as her mother and sisters hurried from the room. She was in for it now, she knew. He hadn't called her *Margaret Ann*, as best she could remember, since last summer, when she had accidentally knocked half a dozen jars of canned green beans off the shelves in the fruit cellar, trying to get away from a black snake.

She sat as still as she could at the table while Da stood watching her, his big arms crossed over his chest. At first Maggie was sure he was going to launch into one of what Eva Grace called his "word-whippings." His face was a thundercloud, and he looked to be working up steam for a fierce scolding.

Maggie braced herself, gripping the chair underneath on either side and trying to swallow down the lump in her throat so she wouldn't shame herself by breaking into a fit of weeping like Baby Ray. But the tongue-lashing for which she steeled herself was slow in coming. Indeed, Da was silent for a long time, though Maggie could feel him watching her.

"All right, now," he finally said, "I think you had best tell me what this is all about, for I'd be willing to wager that you're the one behind this business of a collection."

To Maggie's great relief, his tone, while stern, was no longer angry. Did he really mean to hear her out, then, instead of merely giving her an impatient "piece of his mind," as was usually his way?

Her hopes lifted a little, and she took a deep breath. Perhaps, if she could only make him understand, he would not be so set against the collection.

She chose her words with great care, telling him about the common concern for Mister Stuart—how he had changed, how he looked to be failing, how the loss of his treasured flute seemed to have broken his heart and was draining the life from him. As she spoke, her da slipped quietly onto the chair across from her. He made no attempt to interrupt or disagree, but instead sat ever so still as she went on.

Maggie explained that they had conducted a thorough search for the missing flute but had nothing to show for their efforts but chilblains and briar scratches. She also admitted to being the one who had initiated the idea for the collection.

"Don't you see, Da," she fairly pleaded as she finished her account, "we mustn't lose Mister Stuart from the school. We *need* him. The whole *town* needs him."

Da appeared to be thinking. For a long time, he simply sat in silence, staring at his

hands. Finally, he gave a heavy sigh and looked up. "Maggie, Maggie," he said, shaking his head. "I know you think me a hard man."

He waved away Maggie's attempt to

protest. "You think me hard, and perhaps you are right. But in this case, I'd be the first to agree that your Mister Stuart deserves far better than he got. He is known as a fine man and a good schoolmaster, and he is to be commended for his hard work with you children. 'Tis a shame, what was done to him, and may God have mercy on the black soul of the one who robbed him.

"But don't you understand, girl?" he said, his voice softening even more. "The poor man was not well even before this despicable deed. Why, it's clear to everyone with eyes in their head that your Mister Stuart is in very poor health indeed, and has been for some time."

Maggie started to object, but he stopped her with one large upraised hand. "No, now, listen to me, girl. Mister Stuart was doing poorly when he came to us, and he has shown signs of failing ever since, though I'll admit he has put on a brave show of it throughout. But the man is ill, Maggie. Very ill. And the time has come for you and the other children to accept what cannot be changed.

"Even if by some miracle—and a miracle is what it would take—you managed to collect enough money to replace the flute, I doubt the poor man would have the strength or the breath to play it."

Maggie's heart wrenched at his words.

Again Da shook his head. Watching him, Maggie saw that he no longer looked the slightest bit cross, only sad. Very sad, indeed.

"Ah, Maggie," he said, his voice strangely gentle, "you must face it, lass. There is no more music in the schoolmaster. Your Mister Stuart is in a bad way, don't you see? A hundred silver flutes wouldn't save him now."

The tears Maggie had been choking back finally escaped. She heaved a sob and made to rise from her chair. But Da reached across the table to stop her. "Now, that's the truth of it, Maggie, and you must take it in, once and for all. Even so, girl, your heart is right to want to help, and if I had an extra coin to spare, I would give it to you for your collection. But there is naught, don't you see? There never is. We're a fine big family, and it takes everything the lot of us working together can earn just to make ends meet. I cannot take food from my children's mouths to buy a flute for a dying man. A father cannot do such a thing, girl, and you must not ask me again."

Maggie knew he spoke the truth as he saw it. And hadn't she known all along the response she might expect? But she had also heard her mum say, and often, too, that God could do impossible things. On this occasion, Maggie had allowed herself to hope for the impossible.

Her da patted her hand then, as if to comfort her. At least, Da had been kind and had not mocked her, as he was wont to do sometimes when she riled him. Maggie couldn't remember a time when he had been so gentle with her, so careful of her feelings.

Because of this rare display of tenderness, and because she somehow sensed that he was waiting for a word from her, Maggie managed to tell him that she understood. "I expect what you say is true, Da. I thank you for hearing me out."

He studied her for a moment, then

looked away. "Well ... that's fine then, lass. That's fine." He paused, and when he spoke, his voice had returned to its more familiar gruffness. "Mind, if you can find an odd job or two in addition to your work for the Carlee ladies, you're free to use whatever you earn for your collection. But you're not to be neglecting your schoolwork nor your chores here at home."

Maggie hesitated before getting up to leave the room. Just for a moment she had the oddest feeling that her da was the one who needed comforting instead of herself. She almost thought she had seen a glimpse of the same sorrowful expression in her father's eyes that she had seen of late in Mister Stuart's.

But Da was not a man to admit his feelings. Maggie couldn't quite think of the right thing to say, so after another minute or two, she left the room in silence.

———————————

Even though her family could not give to the collection, Maggie was able to make an extra fifty cents sweeping up the company store two afternoons after school and another half-dollar ironing clothes for the Carlee sisters.

Feeling virtuous entirely, she gave twenty-five cents to her mum from her extra earnings, dropping the remainder in the collection jar. She saw Lily Woodbridge watching when she deposited the coins, and even though Lily had recently made a great show of announcing that her father, Dr. Woodbridge, had contributed ten whole dollars, Maggie felt quite good about her own *contribution*.

She had been somewhat surprised—and disappointed—when Kenny Tallman admitted that his father had scarcely listened to an accounting of their idea before dismissing it as "so much nonsense." He had allowed Kenny only one dollar for the collection, and that grudgingly, from the sound of it.

Even so, Maggie couldn't help but be encouraged by the rising mountain of money in the collection jar; in a week they had collected almost twenty dollars. But she was also keenly aware that they had a long way to go. Why, twenty dollars was probably not even close to what they needed.

To ward off discouragement, she continually reminded herself of the Bible story Mister Stuart had told only this week, about how Jesus had fed an entire crowd with only five loaves and two fish—and still had twelve basketfuls left over! Maggie knew that she and her friends didn't have much chance of raising anything more than what they already had, but if the Lord could multiply bread and fish, He could certainly do the same with a jar of money, couldn't He? If nothing else, perhaps they could find a store that would take their twenty dollars as a down payment on a flute and let them pay the rest on time.

She refused to lose heart. Instead, she continued to pray that God would work in one of those *mysterious* ways her mum was always speaking of and somehow turn their money into music for Mister Stuart.

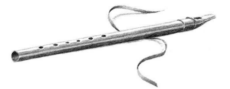

*A*fter two weeks, everyone figured that they had probably collected as much as they were going to, at least for the time being. They had a little more than twenty-five dollars, and although on one hand that amount sounded like a fortune, Maggie wondered if it was even enough to gain entrance to a music store.

A conference was held in the school yard at noon on Thursday. It was decided that the next step should be to learn the actual price of a flute and see if they had raised anywhere near enough money for a down payment.

No one seemed willing to wait any longer in the hopes of accumulating more. They all appeared to be of the same mind— that the sooner they accomplished their goal of presenting Mister Stuart with a new flute, the better, that later might be *too* late. In the meantime, they agreed to look for odd jobs about town to keep money coming in for the flute fund. That way, Maggie pointed out, they would be able to make a payment each month.

The Crawford twins were out of school for the week, helping with their baby brother; without their contrariness, it was easy to reach a unanimous decision on how to proceed. All they needed now was an adult who would be willing to travel to Lexington and make the necessary arrangements.

Lily immediately volunteered her father, pointing out that since he had made the largest *contribution*, it was only right that he be their "agent of purchase." Maggie knew that if Dr. Woodbridge were successful, they would most likely never hear the end of Lily's boasting. On the other hand, she reckoned she could put up with Lily's blather and any number of other annoyances if the doctor managed to bring home a flute for Mister Stuart.

When the bell rang, signaling the end of the noon hour, they entered the school-room in a state of excitement.

Maggie could tell that most of the others were as jittery as she was. The awareness that they were a step closer to fulfilling their plans seemed to stoke them like a furnace. Had Summer been there, at her desk next to Maggie's, no doubt the two of them would have giggled over their shared secret throughout the afternoon. But Summer had been out of school all week, her lung sickness aggravated by the cold rain and sleet of the weekend.

Maggie was rooting among the clutter in her desk for her spelling book when Mister Stuart caught them off guard by rapping his pointer to get their attention. Maggie glanced up, surprised to see that instead of the spelling words the teacher usually wrote on the blackboard during noon hour, there were two names: *Mrs. Hunnicutt* and *The Crawford Family*.

Maggie frowned, wondering what the Widow Hunnicutt, a nice old lady who lived in a log cabin on the hill south of town, had to do with the Crawfords. She looked back to Mister Stuart, who had replaced the pointer and now stood gripping the back of his chair. His knuckles were white, Maggie noticed, as if the mere act of standing required a great deal of effort.

Still, his voice was strong enough when he began to speak. "We have had two special requests today, class," he started in. "One is for the Crawfords—Duril and Dinah's family. The other pertains to Mrs. Alice Hunnicutt. I want to stress that these are urgent needs, and I hope we will do everything we can to help."

The entire class now sat quietly in their seats, intent on the teacher's words and sensing that this afternoon was going to be different from other days.

"Pastor Wallace and Father Maguire stopped by at lunchtime," Mister Stuart went on. "They brought some disturbing news. It seems that the Widow Hunnicutt has suffered a bad fall." His voice held a note of distress as he continued. "Apparently, Mrs. Hunnicutt has been very ill and is ...

malnourished as well."

Maggie felt really bad for Mrs. Hunnicutt, of course, who had always seemed kind, especially to the children in town. She recalled the elderly widow lady coming to visit once, when Maggie's mother had been abed with the pneumonia. Mrs. Hunnicutt had brought them a tasty pandowdy and some of her own blackberry jam.

But what did her misfortune have to do with the Crawfords?

Mister Stuart had paused in his account and now stood looking about the room, his gaze coming to rest on each of them for an instant. "Do you understand what 'malnourished' means, class?"

Lily was the first to reply. "It means the Widow Hunnicutt hasn't been eating right," she said, her tone edged with a hint of reproach.

"It means she's been going *hungry*." Mister Stuart's tone was sharper than usual. He even looked a bit angry, Maggie thought, with more color in his cheeks than had been there for some time.

"It seems that Mrs. Hunnicutt has been without food in the house for several days," he told them. "They found her on the floor of her bedroom. She was sick and hungry—and cold. Her coal bin was completely empty."

Everyone glanced around uneasily. Maggie reckoned they were all of them wondering the same thing: why would anyone's coal bin be empty in a town where coal was mined every day of the week, except on Sundays?

She raised her hand to ask as much but lowered it when Mister Stuart gave a little shake of his head, indicating that she should wait.

"Mrs. Hunnicutt has been taken to the hospital in Lexington for treatment," he said. For a moment he stood studying his desk as if deep in thought. "I don't know about you," he said, looking up, "but I felt ... *ashamed* when I heard about this gracious Christian lady—one of the town's oldest residents—living in such deplorable circumstances. And it seems that things are scarcely better for the

Crawford family. You remember that Duril and Dinah's father was injured in the mine recently?"

A few heads nodded.

"Well, there's a new baby now, and neither the child nor Mrs. Crawford is doing very well. With Mr. Crawford unable to work, there's no money for food and medicine."

Maggie tried hard—truly she did—to feel as sorry for the Crawfords as she did for the Widow Hunnicutt. And she *did* feel bad for them, especially to think that the new baby and Mrs. Crawford might not have enough to eat. But she had to offer up a silent prayer before she could muster an equal measure of sympathy for Duril and Dinah.

When she turned her attention back to Mister Stuart, his face appeared more hollowed, his eyes more deeply shadowed, than ever. "As you know," the teacher continued, "Mrs. Hunnicutt is all alone. Apparently, she has been without funds for some time but didn't want to ask for help. If Pastor Wallace and one of the deacons hadn't called on her when they did ..."

He looked away, and his words drifted over the classroom, unfinished, their meaning unmistakable.

After a moment, he continued. "Pastor Wallace and Father Maguire are asking for donations to stock both Mrs. Hunnicutt's pantry and the Crawfords'. They're also hoping to collect enough to purchase coal and medicine."

Maggie felt just the tiniest twinge of uneasiness somewhere at the back of her mind as Mister Stuart went on. She wasn't quite sure what was nagging at her, but it was an uncomfortable sensation, all the same.

"They understand that no one has a large amount to give," the teacher was saying. "The dropping prices in coal have made for a difficult year. But Mrs. Hunnicutt's situation is most desperate, and so is the Crawfords'. If the town doesn't come to their assistance, the Widow Hunnicutt will probably lose her house and have to go to the county home. And I can't think what will become of the Crawford family."

Maggie looked at her teacher's hands and saw that they were trembling on the back of the chair. "With that in mind," he resumed, "I thought we might take up our own collection here at school. We may not have much, but we can surely contribute something."

He glanced about the room, his gaze stopping to rest on Maggie. "Maggie," he said, smiling for the first time since he had begun to speak, "will you please go to the supply pantry and find a container for us? There ought to be a tray or a jar on the shelves that we can use."

Maggie swallowed and slowly twisted out of her seat. As she trudged down the aisle, she met the wide-eyed stares of some of the other students. In their faces she could see the same troubled questions, the same uneasiness she was feeling.

The collection was almost certain to be a huge failure. No one had any money left, that was the thing. They had given all they had to the collection for Mister Stuart.

Lester Monk was the last to receive the tray. He stared at it for a minute before digging down into first one pocket, then another. He came up empty-handed. Red-faced, he shambled up to the front with the tray in hand.

Mister Stuart had sat down at his desk, but he got up again, smiling as Lester handed him the tray and shuffled back to his seat. As the teacher inspected the tray, however, his smile faded and his features grew taut.

Maggie had known the collection would be scant, but she felt a kind of shame when, after a nerve-racking length of time, Mister Stuart upended the tray, revealing that it was completely empty.

The teacher stood holding the empty tray in one hand while gripping the edge of his desk with the other, all the while regarding them with a look of disappointment that made Maggie wish she could shrink into nothing and disappear.

"It seems—" He cleared his throat as if something were lodged in it. "It seems that we won't be able to help just now." For a long time he said nothing. Then his expression seemed to clear a little. "We can't give what we don't have, of course. But perhaps if we think about it, we might recall having put away some savings to buy Christmas presents. If so, perhaps we'll decide that we can spare at least a little something for Mrs. Hunnicutt and the Crawford family. In the meantime, some of you might consider volunteering to do odd jobs around the Crawford place, and for Mrs. Hunnicutt when she returns home ... if she manages to *keep* her home, that is."

His studying gaze seemed to take in every student in the room, one at a time. "That would be just as good as putting money in a collection, you know—sometimes it might mean even more. When we have no money to give, we can still give something of ourselves—our time, our talents, a word of encouragement, a thoughtful deed. In fact, by giving something of ourselves ... and giving it with love ... we not only give a gift to the other person, but to God as well. I think there can be no finer gift than that."

He smiled at them. "We'll just leave the tray here on my desk for now. Perhaps by

tomorrow, we'll find a little something to put in it."

He flipped open his gold pocket watch then and, after checking the time, turned and began writing the day's spelling words on the blackboard.

As soon as the dismissal bell rang, Maggie and the others lost no time in assembling outside. To make sure Mister Stuart didn't overhear them, they went all the way to the gate at the end of the school yard—and that's where the argument began.

To Maggie's dismay, some of the students seemed to have already made up their minds that the money they had collected ought to go to the Widow Hunnicutt and the Crawfords, rather than toward a new flute for Mister Stuart. Lily Woodbridge quickly moved to squelch the suggestion, and for the first time she could recollect, Maggie found herself in agreement with Lily.

"I positively will not go along with any such thing!" Lily warned, tossing her sausage curls.

Junior Tyree then commenced to make one of the lengthiest speeches Maggie had ever heard leave his mouth. "I reckon we all want to do something for Mister Stuart, but it don't seem right somehow, spending all that money on a music instrument when folks are going hungry." He finished on a quick breath, looking at no one in particular.

"We took up that collection for one reason"—Lily was quick to remind him—"to replace Mister Stuart's flute. The Crawfords and the Widow Hunnicutt are not our concern. We can't be responsible for *everyone*!"

"Especially the Crawfords," someone muttered.

A few heads nodded in agreement.

No one said anything for a moment. Then Kenny Tallman spoke up. "I think Junior's right," he said, pushing his glasses up a little higher on his nose. "It seems like it might be more important to buy food and medicine than a flute—" He paused. "Even if the flute *is* for Mister Stuart."

To Maggie's exasperation, even Lester Monk decided to voice his opinion. "Folks who is hungry need food," he said, his hair standing straight out in the blustery wind. "And sick people can die without medicine."

"Well, Mister Stuart might die, too, if we don't do something!" Maggie blurted out. "We don't have time to start all over again with another collection!"

The instant the words were out, she wished she could swallow them. By a kind of silent agreement, they had been careful not to admit to the fact that Mister Stuart might actually *die*.

Lily didn't seem to notice. "Since my daddy put in almost half of the entire collection, it seems to me I should have some say in what it's used for." Her tone had gone all high pitched by now, the way it always did when she was fixing to take on. "And *I* say it goes toward a new flute for Mister Stuart."

Even though Maggie agreed with her, she sensed that Lily's high-and-mighty airs were rubbing some of the others the wrong way. Hoping to foil a full-blown rucus, she said, "I recommend we go ahead just like we planned. Once we've made a down payment on a flute, we can start up a *new* collection for the Crawfords and Mrs. Hunnicutt."

There was a ripple of approval. But that was before Kenny Tallman spoke up again. "If you don't think there's time to take up another collection for Mister Stuart," he said, not quite meeting Maggie's eyes, "how do you figure the Crawfords and Mrs. Hunnicutt can get by any longer? It sounds to me like they need help right now."

The debate went back and forth from there, but they couldn't seem to settle on anything. At last Kenny suggested they take a vote, and to that much, at least, everyone agreed. It was left that they would get together again first thing the next morning and "vote our conscience—" Kenny's words.

All the way down the road, Maggie puzzled over what her conscience might be trying to tell her. At the same time she wondered how she was going to be absolutely certain she heard it right.

———————

After sweeping up at the company store that same afternoon, Maggie went up on the hill to visit Summer. As always, the Rankin cabin seemed to be running over with people. Maggie reckoned there were more folks crammed into one place here at the Rankins' than anywhere else in town.

She liked visiting Summer. The Rankin house was so crowded and noisy that the two of them could do mostly as they pleased. The grown-ups and little ones were forever chattering at one another, and even though there was usually a baby crying somewhere, there was plenty of laughter as well. There was even music sometimes, on the odd occasion when Mister Rankin picked up his harmonica.

At Summer's house, no one seemed to mind if they tracked mud in from the out-doors or if they left crumbs on the table and silverware in the sink. Moreover, they could drink Mrs. Rankin's strong black coffee instead of milk, and they were allowed to play hidey-go-seek indoors as well as out.

This afternoon, though, Maggie could tell as soon as she arrived that Summer didn't feel up to fun. She found her friend in the back bedroom she shared with her three sisters—a small room separated from the kitchen by a faded blue drape instead of a door. Summer was alone, already hunkered down under a pile of quilts, with nothing showing but her head. Maggie took note of the fiery red stain mottling her friend's face, a sure sign that the fever was on her again.

She sat up the minute she saw Maggie,

though the movement triggered a fit of coughing. Maggie perched on the side of the bed, waiting, trying not to notice the bright red stain on the handkerchief when Summer took it away from her mouth.

"You're feeling bad again, huh?" Maggie asked her.

Summer nodded, then made a face. "Mama says it's because I got caught in the rainstorm." She grinned weakly at Maggie. "She threatened to switch me, but she didn't really mean it, I could tell."

To save her, Maggie couldn't imagine the good-humored Mrs. Rankin taking a switch to Summer—or to anyone else, for that matter. Summer's mother never seemed to get overly cross with her brood, though she had been known to throw a frying pan at *Mister* Rankin now and again, whenever he riled her.

They talked some about school, but Maggie could tell that her friend was feeling more poorly than she let on, so Maggie herself did most of the talking. She waited until last to tell Summer about the plight of the Crawfords and Mrs. Hunnicutt and the failed attempt to take up a collection for them.

Finally, she explained about the vote that was to be taken the next day. Even though it was plain that Summer wouldn't be back in school by then, Maggie asked her opinion on the matter.

"According to Kenny, we have to 'vote our conscience,' " she said. "But I don't rightly know what my conscience is telling me to do. On the one hand, I feel sorry for the Widow Hunnicutt. And though it's kind of hard to feel sorry for Dinah and Duril Crawford, I suppose I wouldn't want their new baby brother going hungry. But the purpose of the collection was to buy a flute for Mister Stuart. And if we don't do it soon—"

She broke off. For the second time that day, she had caught herself thinking that Mister Stuart's time might be limited. Maggie wasn't superstitious—Mum said it was a sin to pay any heed to such pagan notions—but she thought some things were best left unsaid, all the same.

Summer seemed to understand. She

nodded, scooting up a little with her pillows propped behind her.

"So, what do you think?" Maggie asked her directly. "If you were to vote tomorrow, what would you do, do you reckon?"

Summer looked at her, then glanced away, staring at something outside the window. Her fingers plucked at some loose threads on the quilt in a kind of rhythm, over and over again, and Maggie shivered. Picking at the bedclothes was known to be a bad omen indeed. In fact, some of the old folks claimed it was a sign that the end was near.

Shaken, she forced herself to look away. "Well, what do you think?" she asked again, trying for a normal tone of voice. "How would you vote?"

A thought struck her then, and without waiting for Summer's reply, Maggie brought up Mister Stuart's suggestion about "giving something of themselves" instead of money.

"Now, it seems to me," Maggie said, more to herself than to Summer, "that we could use the money to buy a flute for Mister Stuart and do something *else*—like some chores around the house—for Mrs. Hunnicutt and the Crawfords."

She paused. "After all, Mister Stuart

said that 'giving of yourself' can be just as good as giving money—sometimes even better. He said it's like giving God a gift, too."

The more Maggie thought about it, the more she believed she had found the perfect solution. It wasn't as if it was her idea, after all. Mister Stuart was the one who had brought it up in the first place.

Summer turned to look at her. The angry flush to her skin had deepened, and the smudges below her eyes were so dark she appeared to be bruised.

A peculiar feeling came over Maggie, as if someone had poured an icy dipper of water down her back. Without knowing exactly why, she felt afraid. Afraid, and mortal foolish.

The feeling passed when Summer spoke. "I reckon if I was to vote tomorrow," she said, her voice so soft Maggie had to lean forward to hear her better, "I'd first try to figure what Mister Stuart would do."

"What do you mean? Mister Stuart doesn't know anything about the collection."

"But if he *did* know," Summer said,

"what do you think he would tell us to do with it?"

Maggie shrugged, impatient with the question, since it seemed to have nothing at all to do with their present predicament.

Again Summer turned to look out the window. The afternoon light was almost gone and it had begun to snow, large heavy flakes that drifted down like a curtain falling over the gloom of evening.

"Mister Stuart taught us that when we have a hard thing to decide," Summer went on in the same quiet voice, "we should try and figure what Jesus would do. He says that way we won't ever go wrong."

The brief speech seemed to have exhausted her. She closed her eyes. Maggie could hear the wheeze and rattle coming from deep inside Summer's chest, and worried that all the talking might bring on a bad coughing fit.

But after a moment Summer opened her eyes and continued. "I can't always think what Jesus would do. Sometimes I don't even know where to look in my Bible to find out. Those times, I just watch Mister

Stuart real close and try to imagine what *he* would do."

At Maggie's frown, Summer twisted onto her side and moved a little closer to the edge of the bed. "See, I think Mister Stuart lives like Jesus wants *us* to live. Sometimes I almost think I can see Jesus ... living ... in Mister Stuart and looking out from Mister Stuart's eyes. So I reckon if *I* do what I believe Mister Stuart would do ... I can be fairly certain it's the right thing."

Maggie's stomach knotted. Now it was *she* who was plucking at the bedclothes as she watched Summer, who apparently was not quite finished with her answer to Maggie's question.

Her friend looked exceedingly tired and ill, and her voice sounded more raspy than ever as she continued. "I'm pretty sure Mister Stuart would give whatever he had to someone who needed help." Summer smiled then, brightening a little, as if a thought had just occurred to her. "Why, even if we was to give him a brand-new flute, I wouldn't be a bit surprised if he didn't just sell it and give the money to the collection for the Widow

Hunnicutt and the Crawfords."

Summer was still smiling as her eyes fluttered shut. "That's what he would do, I expect … feed the hungry … heal the sick … that's what Mister Stuart would do … Mister Stuart and Jesus.…"

She started coughing then, hard, and they remained silent for a long time. After the coughing finally subsided, Summer seemed to doze, but Maggie didn't leave right away. Instead she sat watching her friend's labored efforts to breathe, thinking about Summer's words.

She knew, deep inside her, that Summer was right. And it made her want to weep. This, then, must be what Mister Stuart had meant when he told them—a long time ago—that doing the right thing wasn't always easy, that it was sometimes very hard indeed, so hard that it might even make a body feel heavyhearted.

That's how Maggie felt at that moment, sitting on the bed beside her sick friend. The reluctant awareness of *the right thing* slowly settled over her. She knew what she ought to do, but the knowing did indeed make her heart feel heavy, much as if it were weighted down by one of the great lumps of coal from deep in the mines.

———————————

As it turned out, the vote planned for the next morning had to be postponed until later in the day. The wet snow of the night before had given way to a freezing rain, making for such a miserable morning, no one wanted to tarry outside.

The dark and dismal day fit Maggie's mood. She slugged through the early classes, attention lagging, her heart still heavy. She hadn't realized until today how much the collection and all the extra activity had occupied her and the entire class and lifted their spirits. The additional odd jobs to raise extra money, the stolen moments of whispered plans had given them all something to look forward to—a spark of excitement in their otherwise dreary routine.

Now all that had changed, and Maggie knew only a leaden sense of defeat and disappointment, coupled with a vague feeling of dread for the days to come. So morose had been her state of mind throughout the morning that she had scarcely noticed anything different about Mister Stuart. It was almost noon before it struck her. The teacher was standing at the blackboard with his pointer, marking off decimal places for Maggie's arithmetic group. After a moment he reached for his pocket watch—and withdrew his hand ... empty. With a slightly baffled expression, he glanced down over his vest. Then his gaze cleared, and he dropped his hand back to his side.

In that moment Maggie knew what had escaped her until now: Mister Stuart's gold pocket watch was gone! She had seen him make the same gesture two or three times throughout the morning, each time with the same reaction.

He had sold it. He had sold his fine gold watch! The sudden realization brought Summer's words of the night before rushing in on Maggie: *"Even if we was to give him a brand-new flute, I wouldn't be a bit surprised if he didn't just sell it and give the money to the collection for the Crawfords and the Widow Hunnicutt...."*

Maggie stared at the teacher as if she had never seen him before. She knew for a certainty that Mister Stuart had sold his gold watch to help the Crawfords and Mrs. Hunnicutt. Summer had been right. She had known what Mister Stuart would do. *"Feed the hungry ... heal the sick ... that's what Mister Stuart would do ... Mister Stuart and Jesus...."*

Maggie sat watching Mister Stuart, and as she did, she began to pray, never mind that she wasn't on her knees and that her eyes were wide open. She prayed that some-how—though she didn't know how in the world such a thing could ever be—she, too, would learn to live like Jesus wanted her to live.

And then, with her heart of hearts, she also prayed that Jesus would let Mister Stuart live—a long, long time.

Please, Lord ... please....

———————

The vote was taken at noon, the weath-er having relented long enough that they could tolerate the outdoors for a brief time.

It went just as Maggie had known it would. Indeed, so certain had she been of the outcome that she had brought the collection jar to school with her that morning.

As soon as she called everyone's attention to Mister Stuart's missing gold watch, they voted—to the last student—to turn the entire amount over to the Crawford family and Mrs. Hunnicutt. There was no arguing about it, no grumbling. Even Lily Woodbridge kept her mouth shut for once. In fact, it was Lily who was appointed to present the money to Mister Stuart on behalf of the class.

If Maggie had had any doubts beforehand, Mister Stuart's response to the collection made it plain as day that they had made the right decision. The instant Lily walked up and thumped the jar down on the teacher's desk—with considerable flourish—Mister Stuart's face brightened with the biggest smile they had seen from him in weeks.

Clearly taken aback, he stared at Lily and the money jar. "Why, Lily, whatever is this?"

At her desk, Maggie held her breath,

hoping Lily would manage to get through her speech before Mister Stuart could ask too many questions.

Lily beamed, and, just as she'd been instructed, proceeded to hurry through an explanation. "This is for the Widow Hunnicutt and the Crawford family," she announced. "It's not from the class alone, of course—we couldn't raise so much money on our own. Our parents helped, too."

Mister Stuart rose from the chair behind his desk and, turning the jar around by its neck, stared at it as if he couldn't believe his eyes. "Why ... why this is wonderful, Lily ... class. I can't think how you managed it, but I am *very* proud of you."

He looked around the room, and for a moment he almost appeared his old self again. He actually seemed happy, Maggie thought, if a bit befuddled.

He lifted the jar then and held it up to the class. "I shall deliver this to Pastor Wallace and Father Maguire this very evening," he said, still smiling broadly. "They will be so pleased and grateful."

Carefully he set the jar down, then

came around his desk to stand in front of the class. "I can't begin to tell you," he said quietly, his gaze stopping for a second or two on each student as he went on, "what this will mean to Mrs. Hunnicutt and the Crawfords. I know it represents a great sacrifice for you and your families, but I know, too, that today you have brought much delight to God's heart. And to mine."

He stopped to clear his throat, and Maggie saw that his eyes had begun to water. He glanced around the room once more, then gave a little nod. "Well … let's get to work now, shall we?"

Was she imagining it, Maggie wondered, or did Mister Stuart have a little more spring to his step when he returned to his desk and began to review the day's spelling words?

As she sat there, only vaguely aware of the teacher at the blackboard, Maggie found herself feeling surprisingly good about the way things had turned out. Despite the fact that they no longer had any hope of restoring the flute that had been stolen, she could tell that they had made

Mister Stuart happy today. She supposed it was a mark of the kind of man he was, that he could sacrifice something as valuable as his gold watch and still be happy—because his students had done something nice for someone else.

With all her heart, Maggie wished there were a way to do something nice for *him*. If only there were a way to give him back his music. If ever a man deserved a special gift, Mister Stuart did.

Well, at least they could give him a party, she suddenly decided. Yes, that's what they would do! They would throw Mister Stuart the best birthday party a body ever had. They would make him a special card, bake him a special cake, and maybe even come up with some sort of special gift. A surprise.

She sat there, ignoring the spelling words, instead pondering what kind of a surprise they might concoct for Mister Stuart's birthday. Again she recalled what the teacher had said to them the day before—about giving something of themselves ... and "giving it with love."

In that moment an idea came over her that made the hair at the back of her neck stand on end—an occurrence that Grandma Vinnie referred to as the "Angel Touch." Maggie had learned from experience that when an idea merited the Angel Touch, it was almost always a fine idea. A dandy of an idea. On occasion, according to her grandma, it might even be a heaven-*sent* idea.

She shook off the chill and started writing notes to herself, hoping Mister Stuart wouldn't call on her just yet. She wanted to get her thoughts down immediately, while they were still foremost in her mind, so she could present them to the others after school.

———————

Maggie's classmates greeted the idea of a surprise birthday party for Mister Stuart with out-and-out enthusiasm. From the moment she related her plan, a renewed wave of excitement swept the group. The fact that there was so much to do in less than ten days only lent an additional edge of eagerness to the undertaking.

All committed themselves to lunch-hour meetings, and, except for a few, each student agreed to try to enlist their parents' help. Those who thought they could get away with it volunteered their houses for special get-togethers as well.

Fired by the others' enthusiasm, Maggie could hardly wait to get to the Rankin cabin to tell Summer. Upon arrival, though, she first reported the news about the vote and Mister Stuart's reaction to the collection. She also confided her suspicion that their teacher had sold his gold watch in order to make his own donation, to which Summer gave a small nod and a smile, as if she weren't in the least surprised.

By the time Maggie had completed an account of the ideas and plans for the party, Summer looked all but exhausted. She leaned back against the pillows with her eyes closed, her thin hands clutching the quilt. An angry red flush stained her hollow cheeks, and her hair was damp from perspiration, although the room was actually cold.

Watching her, Maggie felt a sting of disappointment at her friend's small show of support. But as she studied the frail, unhealthy countenance and the small body that barely made an impression under the bedclothes, she knew Summer's response had nothing to do with lack of interest.

Uneasiness nagged at Maggie, but she forced a cheerful note into her voice. "Now, you absolutely have to get well in a hurry. I'm going to need your help getting everything done proper."

Summer smiled but still didn't open her eyes.

"I mean it now," Maggie said, employing her I'm-older-than-you-so-you-have-to-do-as-I-say tone of voice. "You *have* to be at the birthday party. It will spoil everything if you're not, do you hear?"

Summer opened her eyes, but her reply was cut short by a coughing spasm.

Feeling a little sick herself, Maggie waited. "What will *you* give Mister Stuart for his birthday, do you think?" she asked when Summer was quiet again.

Summer shook her head. "I don't know," she said. "I reckon I'd like to give him something real special. I'll have to think about it."

There was a terrible rasp to her voice, and she was wheezing with a vengeance.

"Well, never mind that for now," Maggie said briskly. "The first thing is for you to get well. We can decide on your gift later. Besides," she said, "I won't actually have anything special to give him either."

Summer looked at her. "That's not true a bit," she said quietly. "You'll be doing the most special thing of all."

Maggie frowned. "I don't know how you figure that."

Summer lifted herself from the pillows and touched Maggie's arm. Her fingers felt scorching hot and dry as paper. "Why, Maggie, you'll be giving the most important gift of anyone. You'll be the one who sees that things get done and everything turns out proper. That's what you do better than anyone else."

That said, she sank back against the pillows again.

"Maybe," Maggie said, feeling a little better.

They were quiet for a time, then Summer turned toward her. "Maggie? I was thinking that maybe we could give Mister Stuart a birthday present from the two of us."

"Like what?"

"I might have an idea. Something that came to mind last night, after I said my prayers."

Maggie looked at her. Summer's eyes were bright and glistening, and Maggie wondered if the fever was rising. "Well, it couldn't cost much," she cautioned. "I only have a few pennies left."

"Me, too. But I bet Junior's daddy would make it for us cheap. He's awful clever with his hands, and he don't charge much. He made new handles for Mama's stove for practically nothing."

Maggie studied her friend, saw the excitement burning in her sunken eyes. "Well?" she prompted, scooting up a little closer on the bed. "So *tell* me."

Summer hesitated. "I'll *show* you," she said. "Ask Mama for some paper...."

———

It was almost dark when Maggie started down the hill for home, Summer's drawing in hand. A light freezing rain was falling, coating the snow from the night before with a slippery glaze, and she had to watch her footing.

Maggie didn't feel as lighthearted as she had upon first hearing Summer's idea for a birthday gift from the two of them. She supposed it was a good enough idea, though she couldn't get nearly as excited about it as Summer had plainly hoped she would be. Nevertheless, she would get Junior to go down to the junkyard with her after school tomorrow and see if his daddy could make something from Summer's drawing.

In truth, she was only going along with Summer because she seemed so set on the idea. Maggie wasn't at all sure what Mister Stuart might think of it.

There was more to her darkening mood, however, than uncertainty about Summer's idea for a gift. An awful ache was upon her, had been gnawing at her most of the evening, and not even the excitement of the birthday party could make it go away.

She stopped once and, without really knowing why, turned to look back up the hill at the Rankin cabin. The lights glowing in the windows made it appear friendly and cheerful, even in the darkness. But then she thought of Summer, who, although surrounded by all the noise and commotion of her family, lay alone in the little back bedroom, feverish and miserable with the coughing.

Maggie was almost home before she realized that the dampness she had been wiping from her eyes most of the way wasn't rain.

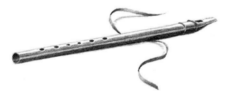

*S*ummer died five days before Mister Stuart's birthday party ... before Amos Tyree could complete the birthday gift from her and Maggie ... and before Maggie had the chance to give her friend the scarlet hair ribbon that was to have been her Christmas present.

It comforted Maggie not a bit that Summer had at least known about the birthday party, had known as well that the present she was so set on giving Mister Stuart was being made according to her wishes.

Maggie had not realized that losing someone she loved would make her feel as though a part of herself had died, too. Along with the cleaving pain that never quite left her day or night, there was a terrible emptiness inside her. She felt as if the bottom had fallen out of her heart and that her deepest dreams and highest hopes were all draining away.

The first thing she thought of every morning was that Summer was gone. At night, when she tried to say her prayers, she still caught herself asking God to make Summer well. Then she would remember and sob the rest of the way through her prayer time.

At school, the empty desk across from her was like a knife, twisting deeper and deeper into her insides. She went on seeing to the details of the birthday party because she didn't know how *not* to go on. But all the plans and preparations, the mounting excitement as the time drew near, seemed to be taking place somewhere outside her and held no reality—and no pleasure.

Without Summer, Maggie seemed to live in a shadow world, where all the lights were dim, and all the rooms were cold, and there was nowhere she could run to get away from the pain. So she carried it with her. Wherever she went, whatever she did, the pain was a constant companion.

The child was inconsolable.

It was too soon for healing, of course, but Jonathan saw no sign that Maggie MacAuley's grief might be easing, even a little. The girl was a shadow of herself, pale and drawn, with a look so solemn, so stricken, it could scarcely be borne.

He had asked her to stay after school in hopes of finding a way to comfort her, or at least to encourage her to talk about her feel-

ings. But now, as the child sat in wooden silence beside his desk, Jonathan felt himself at a loss as to how to begin.

He cleared his throat and tried to give her a bolstering smile. He felt it break and fall apart after the first attempt. "Maggie," he said, hesitating, "I ... thought you might want to talk. About Summer."

She didn't look at him but continued to stare at her hands, knotted into small fists in her lap.

Jonathan groped for the right words, finally giving up and simply saying what was in his heart. "I miss her, too, Maggie. But as much as I miss Summer, I know you miss her even more."

She looked at him. Her eyes were always red-rimmed these days, as if she cried herself to sleep every night.

"Do you want to tell me what you're feeling, Maggie? Would it help to talk about it?"

She shook her head. "I don't reckon anything is going to help."

The voice that usually held such a lilting confidence was dull and thin. Jonathan drew in a long breath, longing for some insight, some shred of wisdom with which to comfort her. But his own heart was so tired and heavy, his own hope so precarious at the moment, he hesitated to speak.

"Maggie ... we'll always miss Summer, but everything she was, everything she did, will always be with us. We never completely lose someone we love, you know."

Abruptly he stopped. The usual bromides would do nothing but insult a child like Maggie MacAuley. She was too astute, too sensitive of spirit, for such banality.

"Are you angry?" he ventured.

Maggie looked at him, and although the green eyes remained guarded, Jonathan thought he detected a spark of something else, a kind of recognition. "Angry?" she repeated.

Jonathan nodded. "With God ... because He didn't heal Summer. I'm sure you asked Him to. I know I did."

Her gaze was steady. "Why didn't He, do you think?"

Behind that simply posed question, Jonathan thought he could hear the cry of the ages. A cry he himself had uttered, and not so long ago.

He gave her the only answer—the only *honest* answer—he was capable of. "I don't know why, Maggie. I don't know. But I wish with all my heart He had."

He saw the tears well up in her eyes in a rush and thought for an instant the child would break into a fit of weeping.

Instead she looked at him straight on. "So do I, Mister Stuart. I wish that more than anything. But since He didn't, I reckon what I have to do now is figure out a way to be getting on. That's what Summer would want me to do." She paused, and again Jonathan saw her control falter as she blinked and looked away. "Summer said I was good at getting things done and making sure everything turns out proper."

It occurred to Jonathan that Summer had known her friend very well. He said nothing, for he felt as if he would strangle on the knot lodged in his throat.

Maggie turned back to him. "I surely wish I could have done that for Summer, Mister Stuart. I wish I could have made everything turn out proper for her."

Jonathan studied the tear-glazed eyes, the taut, strained features, so resolute, yet so vulnerable. "There are some things only God can make turn out right, Maggie. And He *will*. Eventually. He expects us to do the best we can, but He doesn't expect us to do His work for Him."

She rubbed her eyes, then stood. "It helps me a bit to remember that Summer probably isn't coughing anymore. More than likely, she's all well by now, don't you think?"

Jonathan reached for her hand. "Yes, Maggie. I believe with all my heart—and I'm glad you believe it, too—that by now Summer is well and strong, that she's no longer coughing ... but *singing*. Singing with God's angels."

Jonathan could sense her measuring his words. At last she nodded, apparently satisfied with his reply. "Thank you, Mister Stuart," she said solemnly. "I suppose I'll be going on home now."

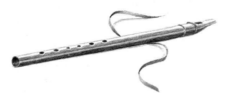

O n the night before his birthday, Jonathan Stuart forced himself to make what was probably the most difficult decision of his life.

For days now, he had been wrestling with a matter that threatened to break his heart every time he confronted it. Tonight he had faced the truth without shrinking, had resigned himself to the reality—and the *finality*—of his deteriorating physical condition, and had somehow come to terms with what he must do.

In the dim solitude of his small study, with an icy, wind-driven snow pelting the windows, despair overcame his spirit as fatigue had overcome his body. So weak had he grown over the past weeks that he virtually dragged himself to and from the schoolhouse each day. The smallest tasks had become trying, to the point that exhaustion had become a way of life for him.

Tonight, after hours of prayer and searching the Word, he could almost believe that he had finally made peace with his war-ring emotions. When the New Year came, he would resign his teaching position at the school. Shortly thereafter, he would leave Skingle Creek.

He felt a grim irony in the fact that he would be retiring from his career at an age when many other men were only setting out on their life vocations. He was a young man; his approaching birthday would see him turn twenty-eight. But he felt as if he had the worn-out heart ... and of late the worn-out spirit ... of an ancient. For weeks now, he had known himself to be failing, and failing badly. The medication wasn't nearly as effective as it had been only a few months past, and the additional hours of rest his Lexington physician had prescribed no longer seemed to make any appreciable difference.

He had been a fool to believe that he could go on as he had been. He was cheating the children; they deserved a teacher who was fit and strong, healthy enough to do the job as it ought to be done. It simply wasn't right to delay any longer.

He had already decided that he wouldn't return to his family home. He had no intention of putting his parents through the grief of watching him die. Nor would he have his students remember him as a dying man. There was a place the doctor in Lexington had told him about—a kind of sanitarium, where those with serious illnesses could go, supposedly for continuous treatment and rest. Jonathan suspected that in truth it was more a retreat where the hopelessly ill could await the end.

He had to face the fact that finances could be a problem. Because his teaching salary was spare, to say the least, he had managed to accumulate very little in the way of savings. And with both his flute and his gold watch gone, he no longer had anything of any real value to sell.

But God had been faithful in the past to take care of his financial needs; he would simply have to trust Him to do so in the future. He sighed, wringing his hands, as he began once more to search through his Bible for comfort or at least some word of affirmation. For even with his decision settled, the peace he sought still eluded him, especially when he thought about leaving his students.

His children.

He knew they would be far better off with a teacher who wasn't ill and weak from fatigue most of the time. Still, he found himself riddled with doubts and an excruciating sadness. He had prayed and searched the Scriptures most of the evening for some assurance that would put his mind and heart at rest; instead, he found himself growing more confused than ever about what, exactly, God might be trying to say to him.

My strength and my hope have perished from the Lord ... my soul melts from heaviness; strengthen me according to Your word.

But just what was God's "word" for him? Puzzled, Jonathan flipped through the pages, staring at the passage to which his reading had taken him:

This I recall to my mind, therefore I have

hope. Through the Lord's mercies we are not
consumed, because His compassions fail not.
They are new every morning; great is Your
faithfulness. The Lord is my portion, says my
soul; therefore I hope in Him!

Hope? Jonathan removed his glasses and
rubbed a hand over his eyes. How long had
it been since he had felt any real hope, other
than the ultimate hope of heaven?

And yet he had always hoped in the
Lord—in His goodness, His love, His
promises. And he *still* hoped in Him.

Didn't he?

After a moment he replaced his reading
glasses and renewed his search, thumbing
through His Bible as if an unseen hand were
guiding him.

For I know the thoughts that I think toward
you, says the Lord, thoughts of peace, and not
of evil, to give you a future and a hope.

A future? And a hope? "Dear Lord, I
have resigned myself to the fact that I most
likely *have* no future ... except eternity with
You," Jonathan whispered. "And I am at
peace with that. I *am*."

Have you not known? Have you not heard? The everlasting God, the Lord, the Creator of the ends of the earth, neither faints nor is weary.... He gives power to the weak; and to those who have no might He increases strength ... those who wait on the Lord shall renew their strength; they shall mount up with wings like eagles, they shall run and not be weary; they shall walk and not faint.

Jonathan felt a sudden stirring in his spirit, a kind of breathless expectancy. He was only vaguely aware that he was trembling, his tired heart racing. Confusion merged with anticipation, and he found himself wholly caught up in the Word of God as he had not been in weeks, perhaps in months.

The Lord is my strength and my song....

But he *had* no strength. And the song of his soul seemed long forgotten.

He has put a new song in my mouth....

A *new* song? But he had *no* song. There was no longer any music in him.

His singing voice had always been a disappointment to him at best. But as long as he had had his flute, he had never minded his inadequate voice all that much. The praise and joy of his heart had found a clear and shimmering voice in the golden notes of his flute. Most mornings, and evenings, too, he had let the music of his soul pour

forth in unconstrained melodies of praise. The very act had been as much a part of his worship as the hymn singing on Sunday mornings and his prayer and Scripture study at night.

But the flute was gone, and with it,

every vestige of his music.

The Lord is my strength and my song....

Jonathan's eyes locked on the verse he had read only moments before. He read it again. And again.

His hands were shaking on the fragile pages of the Bible. Carefully, he removed his glasses that the tears might flow freely.

And then, still questioning, still seeking, he went to his knees. He made no petition, neither for himself nor for others. He did not plead. He did not speak. He scarcely breathed. He merely waited in the silence, listening.

Much later—he could not have said *how* much later—Jonathan saw again, as if before him, the same words of conviction and promise. He saw them, heard them, felt them reverberate throughout his entire being as though plucked on the strings of his spirit:

The Lord is my strength and my song....

A wave of awareness, like the dawn coming up over the fog-veiled valley after a seemingly endless night, rose up in him. And in his spirit, Truth whispered:

THE MUSIC OF LIFE IS WITHIN YOU, JONATHAN. NOT IN THE WORLD, NOT IN CIRCUMSTANCES OR EXTERNAL THINGS ... AND NOT IN AN INSTRUMENT. YOU ARE THE INSTRUMENT, AND I AM THE MUSIC. WHATEVER ROAD YOU WALK IN THIS LIFE, IT IS BECAUSE I HAVE SET YOUR FEET UPON IT. WHATEVER TRIALS YOU ENCOUNTER, WHATEVER STRUGGLES YOU ENDURE, YOUR JOYS, YOUR SORROWS ... THESE, TOO, ARE MY WILL. I WOULD HAVE YOU, THROUGH THE LIFE YOU LIVE WITH ME, SHOW THESE CHILDREN ... THESE PEOPLE ... THAT THE MUSIC OF LIFE IS WITHIN, NOT WITHOUT ... THAT IT COMES FROM ME. I AM YOUR HOPE ... YOUR STRENGTH ... YOUR SONG. I, THE LORD, AM YOUR MUSIC.

It was almost first light on the morning of his birthday when, for the first time in a very long time, Jonathan Stuart lifted his hands toward heaven and began to praise his Creator-Father God with a melody only the soul can sing.

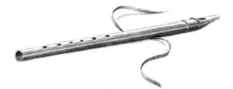

On the evening of Mister Stuart's birthday party, the students and their parents arrived well ahead of time, as Maggie had requested. Her mum and older sisters had brought the cake in earlier, setting it up to display nicely with the lemon punch that Mrs. Woodbridge had made.

To Maggie, it was an odd sight entirely to see Mum working alongside Lily's mother, the two of them being from opposite sides of town and probably having never brushed elbows before tonight. Maggie couldn't help but notice that Mrs. Woodbridge actually seemed much kinder and sweeter-faced up close than she appeared from a distance.

In truth, more than one parent had surprised her, including her own. It was as if something had happened among the grown-ups, something altogether unexpected. Once they learned how hard the children at the school had worked on the collection for Mister Stuart—only to give it up for a "greater need"—they had begun to pitch in and do whatever they could to help: gathering clothes and food and additional funds for the needy of the community, as well as lending their efforts to the birthday party.

From what Maggie had heard, most of the families in town had decided to donate what little they might have spent on Christmas presents for themselves to help families like the Crawfords and the Widow Hunnicutt. And it seemed that *everyone* had turned out tonight for Mister Stuart's birthday party. Even Judson Tallman, Kenny's father, had shown up—and with candy and fruit for all the students!

Knowing this, Maggie couldn't help but feel that maybe things had worked out for the best, after all. Yet her heart was still burdened by sorrow, for without Summer to share in the good things that were happening, there was no real excitement or joy for her, either.

She reminded herself that she still had things to do before Mister Stuart arrived. She found her da, and the two of them moved the teacher's desk and chair to the very front and center of the room, not only to make more space for the party, but also to afford the guest of honor a clearer view.

As always, Mister Stuart's desk was neat and orderly, with only two or three books propped up on one side, a cup of pencils and the attendance register on the other. Maggie placed the handmade birthday cards from the students and their families on the desk, then stepped back. As she stood inspecting her work, she clutched the brown paper-wrapped gift to her heart, as if its contents might somehow bring her absent friend closer tonight. When her vision blurred, she turned away and went to give the others their last-minute reminders, still holding the birthday gift closely to her.

Finally, there was nothing left to do except to wait for Mister Stuart's arrival.

Maggie caught her breath when she

saw Pastor Wallace step inside the darkened schoolroom, pausing to hold a lantern aloft. The plan was that the pastor would invite Mister Stuart out for a birthday supper, but suggest that they first stop by the school to borrow some paper and paint for the church's Christmas pageant.

On cue, those parents who had earlier been assigned the task now hurried to light oil lamps and lanterns, setting some in place, holding others. For a moment Maggie was afraid something had gone wrong and Mister Stuart hadn't come. But then the teacher appeared, framed in the doorway before advancing the rest of the way over the threshold.

As he walked in, the schoolroom filled with light, and everyone cried out a greeting in unison:

"Happy birthday, Mister Stuart!"

Maggie's heaviness lifted a little when she saw the teacher's face. Obviously, they had pulled off the surprise—he was clearly stunned. Laughter broke out around the room, then applause, as Mister Stuart stood gaping at them.

They continued to applaud as Pastor Wallace patted him on the back and led him toward the front of the room to his desk. Mister Stuart turned to face them with a baffled smile. He appeared, Maggie noticed, greatly flustered, as if embarrassed by such attention.

The applause finally subsided, and Pastor Wallace began to speak.

Jonathan heard only scattered fragments of Pastor Wallace's greeting, but enough to realize that apparently all this was for him. He found the idea nothing short of astounding! The small schoolroom was crammed with what appeared to be all his students and their families, plus numerous other members of the community as well. There was even a table with a cake and refreshments. And, in the far corner, a varied array of musical instruments!

Every face in the room seemed to be smiling at him with good-natured enjoyment at his surprise. He saw the crowd of well-wishers through a thin haze, as if he stood at a great distance from them, watching them through heat rising from the ground.

Years of teaching had instilled in him the ability to assess and analyze—then react—rather quickly. But, at the moment, Jonathan was having difficulty focusing, much less trying to form an appropriate response. He felt almost dizzy and a little disoriented.

But through the fog of bewilderment, he heard enough of Ben Wallace's address to understand that the children had planned all of this—the entire party—in his behalf, enlisting the help of their parents as needed. Without his knowing it, there had apparently been some speculation about his health, perhaps even about his staying in town, for Pastor Wallace had much to say about how the community appreciated Jonathan, and that they were hopeful he would see fit to stay in Skingle Creek "for a long, long time." There was mention of his efforts on the children's behalf, efforts that had "benefited the entire community"—and, finally, an explanation that his students were desirous of giving him "a very special birthday gift" ... a gift of *music*.

Jonathan blinked at Pastor Wallace's closing words, watching as Maggie MacAuley, her face still ravaged by her recent loss, stepped up. She gave Jonathan a brave smile, then began to speak, precisely and clearly, as if her words had been well rehearsed. "The class wanted you to know how sorry we are about what happened to your flute, Mister Stuart."

Jonathan's head finally began to clear. He studied the little redheaded girl standing so straight in front of him, clutching a brown paper package tightly against her as if she feared someone might attempt to tear it from her arms.

"We took up a collection some time back," she went on, "hoping to buy you a *new* flute and give you back your music. But when we heard about Mrs. Hunnicutt—" She stopped, darting a glance around the schoolroom. Jonathan had already seen the Crawfords among the crowd; to Maggie's credit, she didn't mention their names.

"When we heard about ... those who needed help," she continued, "we decided the
collection should go to them."

She paused. "We thought that's what
you would want us to do, if we were to ask."

*The collection. The jar they had filled with
money overnight....*

A knot swelled in his throat as Maggie
went on, squeezing the words together in a
rush, as if to get them all out before she forgot anything. "Since we couldn't replace
your flute, we tried to figure a way we could
still give you back your music." She stopped
and caught a breath. "And, well ... that's
our birthday gift to you tonight. So if you'll
just sit down, please, Mister Stuart, we'll be
getting started now."

Poor, sad little wren, her heart was still
aching over Summer, Jonathan knew. He
smiled into her eyes, hoping to encourage
her, then seated himself.

Lily Woodbridge came up next, a paper
in hand. She gave Jonathan a big, expectant
smile, then shot Maggie a look that clearly
said they were to trade places.

With a stiff little nod in Jonathan's

direction, Maggie scurried off into the crowd, still clutching the brown parcel to her heart.

Jonathan found himself wondering what could be in the package Maggie was guarding with such diligence. But he had no time for further conjecture, for just then Lily commenced her role as announcer, and the party began.

If Jonathan had thought himself amazed at the beginning of the evening, by the time the "third gift" had been presented, he was positively overwhelmed. So far, he had been treated to a trio composed of Maggie's father, Matthew MacAuley, on the melodeon; Amos Tyree, on the banjo; and Amos's son, Junior, on the "bones." Next, Dr. Woodbridge had rendered a somewhat nervous but surprisingly sweet tenor solo of "Barbara Allen." And Caleb Crawford had stumbled up to the front on crutches to shake the tambourine, while his twins Dinah and Duril offered, if not an entirely melodic, at least a *lively* vocal duet of "Camptown Races."

It was a veritable delight for Jonathan to see the boisterous twins actually taking part in something besides trouble. It was even more satisfying to see their father sober on a Friday night.

As the evening wore on, he felt himself almost overcome with a kind of paternal pride and pleasure. To see his students exercising such an impressive display of talent, and to realize that they were offering it all to him as a gift, made his heart swell nearly to bursting. Truly, tonight was the finest gift he had ever received. He could not imagine anything ever surpassing it.

The only disappointing moments of the entire evening came when he happened to glance at Maggie MacAuley's drawn, unsmiling countenance. She stood near the front, watchful and heartbreakingly solemn, holding her precious package—for surely it must be *very* precious to the child, judging from the way she was guarding it—and looking as if at any moment she might run from the room weeping. Without the customary twinkle in her eye and the slightly tilted smile, the girl looked much too old ... and far too sad ... for her years.

Knowing Maggie as he did, Jonathan surmised that she had been the instigator of this entire event, but was finding it nearly impossible to enjoy without her friend Summer here to share it with her. With all his heart, Jonathan wished he could give *Maggie* a gift tonight—a gift that would somehow return the light to her eyes and the smile to her face.

He was wrested from his reflection by a stirring in the crowd. As he watched, the students—every one of them, as best he could tell—stepped up to form two rows just in front of him. At the same time, Dr. Woodbridge came forward and, after a quick nod and a quirk of a smile, turned to direct this unique choir in Foster's "Hard Times," followed by Jonathan's favorite hymn, "Amazing Grace."

Jonathan felt close to choking on the emotion that welled up in him. Those same feelings very nearly overpowered him as Herb Rankin, Summer's father—who had been standing directly behind the children—plucked his harmonica from his shirt pocket and began to accompany the hymn.

Jonathan had been surprised, and exceedingly moved, when he realized that Summer's parents were in attendance tonight. Now as he stood watching the children and Herb, whose grief was still so sharply etched upon his gaunt face, the pain of his loss so achingly apparent in the lonely wail of the harmonica, it was all he could do to maintain his composure.

Yet in the midst of his turbulent emotions, he was acutely aware of the words of the stirring old hymn as the children's sweet, albeit imperfect, voices filled the schoolroom:

The Lord has promised good to me,
His word my hope secures;

He will my shield and portion be
As long as life endures.

Jonathan stood there, the words and music penetrating to his very soul as he looked out upon the unlikely group of grown-ups and young people who had come together to give to *him* on this evening of his birthday. In that moment he was moved with such love and gratitude he simply could not contain it. Tears began to track his face, and while such an unrestrained display of emotion would have embarrassed him at any other time, tonight he was scarcely aware of it.

> *Through many dangers, toils and snares*
> *I have already come;*
>
> *'Tis grace hath brought me safe thus far,*
> *and grace will lead me home.*

When the last stanza had ended, the children stood quietly as Herb Rankin went on playing the melody through again. The harmonica no longer keened but seemed to soar in a solitary affirmation of faith and hope and a kind of triumph.

At last the music ended. The children and Herb Rankin dispersed, melding with the others. Jonathan drew a deep, unsteady breath. Sensing the end of the evening at hand and knowing he might be expected to say something—as he certainly ought to, of course—he got to his feet.

But instead of Lily moving to close the program, Maggie MacAuley now walked up to stand in front of him once again. The child's eyes were red and shadowed, her smile somewhat uncertain, and she still hugged the brown paper package to her heart.

For a moment she stood staring up at Jonathan. Then, in a gesture as protective as if she were handing him a valuable family heirloom, she extended the parcel to him. "This is for you, Mister Stuart," she said, her voice pitched low. "From Summer and me, the two of us. I'm not one bit musical, you see, and since Summer couldn't be here ..."

For an instant her face threatened to crumple, and Jonathan reached out a hand to steady her. But after a moment the sharp little chin lifted and she went on. "It was all Summer's idea ... the gift was, I mean. I just wanted to make sure you understood that it's from both of us ... but mostly from Summer."

The girl practically shoved the package into Jonathan's hands but made no move to leave; instead, she stood watching him with unnerving intensity. Jonathan looked from Maggie to the parcel. His hands were shaking badly as he loosened the string and carefully removed the paper wrapping. His throat threatened to close, and he was trembling so that he had to place the box on top of the desk before he could go on.

He glanced at Maggie. Her gaze seemed locked on his hands as he opened the lid of the box and examined the contents.

Maggie drew a long sigh of relief and satisfaction to finally see the birthday gift safely in Mister Stuart's possession. Her mother had helped her to wrap it, had even used a scrap of silk from her sewing box. She thought Summer would have approved of their efforts.

She watched Mister Stuart closely, trying to measure his response. But his expression was hard to read, as if perhaps he were trying to sort out his feelings.

It occurred to Maggie that she had forgotten to mention something. "Mister Stuart?"

He straightened and looked at her in a most peculiar way. Maggie saw that his eyes were glazed with tears, but she didn't think they were unhappy tears, for his face appeared to be shining.

"You should know that Amos Tyree—Junior's daddy—made it from a picture Summer drew. He worked real hard to get it exactly right."

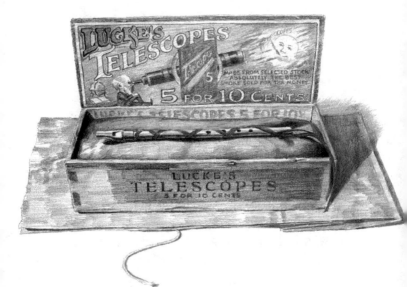

Mister Stuart looked at her, then back at the open box. He lifted a hand and wiped it across his eyes, then gave a small nod and bent his head over the gift.

Jonathan's heart threatened to explode from his chest as he finally managed to take in what had to be the most unusual—and the most precious—birthday gift he had ever received.

Cradled on what appeared to be a small doll's pillow that had been covered in shiny green fabric rested a bright new tin whistle—a penny whistle. To Jonathan's tearful eyes, the primitive instrument resembled his missing flute. He wondered at the piece of scarlet ribbon that had been threaded lovingly around the tin whistle.

After a long moment in which he struggled to get his breath, Jonathan removed the penny whistle from the box, complete with its emerald green pillow and scarlet ribbon, and carefully extended it toward the parents and students. "A gift from Maggie MacAuley... and Summer Rankin," he choked out.

There was a collective intake of breath among the students and their families, followed by some speculative murmurs. Then a hush fell over the entire schoolroom as everyone watched Jonathan ... and waited.

———————

Had he ever played a penny whistle before tonight?

Jonathan couldn't remember. Perhaps, when he was a boy. He thought he could manage. The technique shouldn't be all that different from playing the flute, after all.

More to the point, did he have the breath or the strength to play it?

He must. He must do this, at least once. For the little girl with the wounded, watchful eyes—for Maggie. And for the one who was very much with them tonight, in their hearts—for Summer. He wanted to play for all of them—his children ... his people ... his family.

AND FOR ME, JONATHAN ... PLAY FOR ME. *Give me the strength. Lord....*

I AM YOUR STRENGTH, JONATHAN ... REMEMBER? I AM YOUR STRENGTH AND YOUR SONG.

With painstaking care, Jonathan lifted the penny whistle from its pillow, and, after unwinding the scarlet ribbon from around it, brought the instrument to his lips.

One steadying breath. And then he began to play ... tentatively, at first, then with mounting confidence. For a moment, he did not realize that his breath was coming in a pure, fresh rush, or that his strength was increasing, new and flowing, as if a well had been uncapped from which he was free to draw all he wanted, all he needed. He was conscious only of the music trilling from the penny whistle.

And yet it *wasn't* coming from the penny whistle, not really, for surely the narrow little instrument was pitifully inadequate for the pure, golden notes that cascaded from it, sweeping and soaring over the room. No, the music seemed to be coming from his *heart* ... from his *soul*. It was new—a new song—each note bubbling up and spilling out from him, only to be caught by the penny whistle and flung out to all those in the room. Even as he played, God's love for him—and his for God and every person in the schoolroom—was transposed into the music.

What had begun as a gift to *him*—to Jonathan—now became a gift *from* him—to his students and their families. A gift poured out with indescribable love and turned to something of glory by the Giver of *all* gifts.

Jonathan closed his eyes and played on, lost now in this glorious music he knew had little to do with the instrument or with himself, but everything to do with the One for whom he played.

He has put a new song in my mouth....
The Lord is my strength and my song....

AND YOU WILL SING THAT NEW SONG AND PLAY THE MUSIC I GIVE YOU, JONATHAN, FOR AS LONG AS I WILL THAT YOU DO SO. I WAS WITH YOU AT THE BEGINNING OF YOUR JOURNEY, AND I WILL BE WITH YOU UNTIL YOUR JOURNEY'S END. YOUR DAYS, YOUR TIMES, ARE IN MY HANDS.

Jonathan went on playing, his eyes open now. He saw the stares of wonder and astonishment, mingled with love, fixed upon him. He felt the wonder and amazement inside himself, and at the same time, received the love of the people and offered them his, along with the music.

*For I know the thoughts that I think toward
you, says the Lord, thoughts of peace and not
of evil, to give you a future and a hope.*

A FUTURE AND A HOPE FOR YOU ... AND
FOR THESE, YOUR PEOPLE AND MINE. SO PLAY
ON, JONATHAN. PLAY YOUR MUSIC. MY
MUSIC. SING YOUR NEW SONG. FOR I AM
YOUR HOPE, YOUR STRENGTH, YOUR SONG.
I, THE LORD, AM YOUR MUSIC.

———————————

Maggie had slipped back into the
crowd the minute she saw that Mister
Stuart meant to play the penny whistle.
Watching him, she thought he might be
praying, for his eyes were closed as he
played a kind of music she had never heard
before. It was the most beautiful, rare, and
glorious music! Indeed, the penny whistle
didn't sound as if it had been made from a
sheet of junkyard tin at all, but more as if it
had been crafted of the finest silver, fash-
ioned by the very hands of God's angels.

*Summer ... Summer, can you hear? Mister
Stuart is playing the penny whistle, and the*

music is a glory, a wondrous thing entirely! He's playing for us, Summer, and the music is more grand than anything he ever played on his expensive silver flute! Oh, Summer, I hope you can hear it, all the way up into heaven. I hope you can hear it!

Maggie could not think how such a small and simple thing as the homemade penny whistle could give forth such sound—like a pure crystal sea of heavenly music!

And then Mister Stuart opened his eyes and looked directly at her as he went on playing. Maggie suddenly realized that she was weeping, but at the same time smiling through her tears ... smiling and almost laughing aloud at the new joy and strength ... and *hope* she could see shining in Mister Stuart's eyes as he played, a hope that seemed to reach out and draw her in, along with her family and everyone else in the schoolroom. It was as if God were putting His arms around them all.

The penny whistle itself looked to be aglow. It had caught the light from all the lamps in the schoolroom, and now it blazed and shimmered like pure silver as it dipped and rose in Mister Stuart's hands. And for the first time in what had seemed like an endless age, Maggie could feel the music washing away the coal dust and grime from Skingle Creek. The town ... and her heart ... were being washed clean of their dust and pain and sorrow—cleansed and made new by the music from Mister Stuart's penny whistle ... *and God's love.*

In that moment, Maggie MacAuley knew that the music had come back to Skingle Creek, this time to stay.

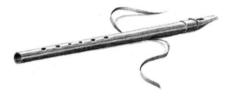

Fifteen years later

It was June in Kentucky. The air was warm and sweet-scented with wild flowers and the rich, pungent fragrance of newly mown grass and freshly turned earth.

With classes now dismissed for the summer, the school yard was empty and unnervingly quiet. The schoolhouse looked much as she remembered it, except that a new wing had been added. But the siding was the original white clapboard, which looked to have been recently painted, and the bell still hung suspended from the iron frame near the steps. The old rusting gate had also been replaced, this one wider, with hinges that didn't creak when she opened it.

Because of the travel expense and her lack of free time, her visits home had been few and far between over the years. Once before, she had come to the schoolhouse, only to find it empty. Because of flood damage, the children were being transported by wagon to the school in Fletcher. She had tried again, years later, but that time he had been away in Lexington, visiting his parents.

Over the years her mother had written of the additions to the schoolhouse, keeping pace with the moderate growth of the town. Somehow she had expected a more drastic change. But other than the new wing, the building appeared the same plain but sturdy structure she remembered from her childhood.

As she followed the path up the school yard, she could almost hear her own childish voice mingling with others from the past. Without warning, memories came rushing in on her like a summer storm, long-forgotten images of an earlier, simpler time she had foolishly thought would go on forever.

Where were the others now, she wondered?

Some she had kept in touch with, at least during the early years. Later, her mother's letters had brought her occasional news of them. Kenny Tallman, to everyone's surprise and no doubt his father's despair, had gone to the mission field. He was reported to be somewhere in South America. Junior Tyree, in partnership with his father, had started a lumber mill outside of town and, last she'd heard, had become relatively prosperous. Poor Lester Monk had died in the worst mine accident in the history of the county—the same accident that had lamed her father. Lester had died a hero, saving the life of another miner. As for Lily Woodbridge—and now she was able to smile again—Lily had decided early on, before they ever graduated from high school, that she would become a nurse and marry a doctor, in that order. True to form, she had accomplished both.

By now she had reached the front doors of the schoolhouse, which stood open in invitation to the balmy weather. As if the sound of her footsteps might somehow intrude upon the past, she found herself walking on tiptoes.

She saw him immediately. He was sitting at a desk—the same desk he had used fifteen years ago, she was certain—writing. She remembered the fine hand that had graded her papers so carefully, the precise script, the slight, unexpected flourish with which he crossed the final "t" of his name.

Even though she had known he would be here, she was completely unprepared for the emotion that welled up in her at the sight of him. The head bent over the desk was still flaxen, though in places strands of silver caught the light. His glasses had slid down on his nose a little, and he appeared to be deep in thought as his pen scraped the paper.

She heard him sigh, and she couldn't help but smile. He had often sighed back then, too, most usually when faced with a particularly inadequate test paper.

She was about to knock when he looked up. His expression was questioning but pleasant, a smile forming quickly.

For a moment she found herself unable

to speak. Only now did she realize how very young he had been all those years ago. Why, he was *still* a young man. He hadn't been old at all back then, but ill—terribly ill.

Obviously, that was no longer the case. The lean face was warm with the glow of health, the eyes behind his spectacles alight with the same keen intelligence and kindness, the same faint glint of humor she remembered.

Ever the gentleman, he got to his feet. "Yes, may I help you?"

For some ridiculous reason, Maggie's eyes started to fill. She blinked, then blinked again as she slowly walked the rest of the way into the room. "Hello, Mister Stuart," she managed to say.

He inclined his head to one side a little, regarding her closely.

It gave Maggie an inordinate amount of pleasure to see his expression gradually change from curiosity to recognition, then delight. "*Maggie?* Why it is, isn't it? Maggie MacAuley!"

He came around the desk to greet her.

Maggie clasped his hand, which was warm and strong—stronger than she might have expected—and all at once she was laughing. It was just so good, so incredibly good, to *see* him again, to hear him call her "Maggie" again. Over the years she had become "Meg" to her friends. But she had never quite left "Maggie" behind.

"I'm so glad to see you, Mister Stuart," she said, only then releasing his hand.

"Well . . . Maggie!" He studied her openly, shaking his head as if he couldn't believe his eyes. "Goodness, you make me feel old!"

Maggie laughed. "And you, Mister Stuart, make me feel young again. But how did you recognize me so quickly?"

Still smiling, his glance flicked to her untamed red hair. Maggie rolled her eyes and nodded.

He motioned for her to take the chair near the desk. "I want to hear everything about you," he said, waiting for her to sit down before returning to his own chair across from her. "I see your mother and father occasionally, you know. I've kept in touch as well as I could through them."

"Then, you know I'm a teacher."

He positively beamed in reply. "And, I'm quite sure, a very *good* one."

Maggie grinned at him. "As a matter of fact, I *am,* Mister Stuart. But then I had a fine example as my inspiration." She paused. "Not to mention the scholarships you made possible for me."

He shook his head. "The scholarships were entirely your doing, Maggie. You were bright, and you worked hard. All I did was submit your name and your records."

"You made two trips to Cincinnati on my behalf," she said quietly. "I know all about it."

They talked for a long time. As always, he spoke little about himself, instead plying Maggie with questions about her life, then leaning forward with great interest as she told him.

At one point Maggie found herself wondering why Jonathan Stuart had never married. According to her mother, there had never been anyone in his life. The common assumption was that it had to do with his poor health, but Maggie wasn't so sure. The man across the desk from her looked anything but unhealthy.

No, she thought it more likely that he had simply given his life to the school, to the children. *His* children, he had always called them.

"Mother wrote me that you're the principal now," Maggie said. "It's hard for me to think of you not teaching."

"Oh, I still teach," he assured her. "We can't afford a full-time principal. To tell you the truth, I don't really *like* the job all that much. I prefer the classroom. But they couldn't seem to find anyone else, and I was here, so—" He shrugged, smiling. "But I want to know more about you, Maggie. You're living in Chicago now, your mother told me. And working with one of the immigrant societies. Is that in addition to your teaching?"

"Actually, it's a part of it. I work at a settlement house," Maggie explained. "Hull House, it's called. I trained under Miss Jane Addams, the founder. Mostly I teach immigrant children. And I teach classes on citizenship for their parents as well."

He favored her with a look of approval. "I always knew you would do something special with your life. And I wasn't in the least surprised when I learned you were working with children. You were always so good with the younger students in the classroom."

He seemed to hesitate for a moment. "I often think of Summer. I imagine you do, too."

Again Maggie nodded. "I wrote a story about her last year," she confided to him. "It's to be published as a children's book in a few months."

"Oh, Maggie, how wonderful! I hope you'll send me one of the first copies off the press."

Maggie assured him that she would. She didn't mention the fact, however, that the book carried a dedication to him. Or that it was entitled *The Penny Whistle*. She thought she would let that remain a surprise.

She decided then to ask him the question she had wanted to ask for years.

"Mister Stuart? I've often wondered ... did you ever find your silver flute?"

He smiled a little, then shook his head. "No," he said quietly, looking away, "I never did."

Maggie murmured a sound of disappointment.

But when he turned back to her, she was surprised to see that his face seemed radiant. "It doesn't matter," he told her. "In fact, I think it's best that I never learned what happened to the flute."

Puzzled, Maggie frowned.

He pointed then to the wall behind her, and slowly she turned to look. Until now, she hadn't seen the small, glass-enclosed cabinet fastened to the wall. There, behind the glass door, still resting on the small green pillow and draped with the scarlet ribbon, was the penny whistle she and Summer had given him so many years ago.

Tears scalded Maggie's eyes as she finally dragged her gaze away from the display case and turned to face Jonathan Stuart.

"The penny whistle has meant so much

more to me than the flute ever could have," he said. "It changed my life." After a moment, he added, "I think perhaps it may have *saved* my life."

He rose and walked over to the window, where he stood, hands clasped behind him, looking out in silence. Finally he turned back, volunteering the answer to Maggie's unspoken question. "I still play it, you know," he said. "I play it for the children, for each new class at the beginning of every school term—and on special occasions during the year. And when I play, I tell them a story. A story about two very special young friends who gave their teacher a precious gift from God."

Maggie swallowed. "Mister Stuart? What … really happened that night, with the penny whistle? I've never understood."

He removed his glasses and stood studying her for a moment. "What happened, Maggie," he finally replied, "was *hope*. That was your gift … yours and Summer's … to me. In your innocent, unselfish desire to help me, you actually enabled me to find my hope again."

He paused, and when he went on, Maggie almost had the sense that he was speaking more to himself than to her. "It's strange, but I can still remember that, as a young teacher here in Skingle Creek, the need I sensed most in the children was the need for *hope*. I resolved to somehow *give* them that hope. Yet, as it turned out, it was the children who ultimately restored the gift of hope to *me*."

He passed a hand over his eyes, then replaced his glasses. "That winter was a terrible time for me. I was all but dead, at least in my spirit. For the most part, I was simply waiting for the end. At first, I attributed this … deadness … to my illness. Later, I somehow came to rationalize that it was a direct result of losing the flute. Music had always been such a-a *necessary* thing to me, you see. It was almost as if the absence of my music—or perhaps my inability to *make* music—was responsible for my decline."

He shook his head, his faint smile rueful. "I was so terribly, terribly wrong. It was the absence of *hope* that had stolen my music, not the loss of the flute. I was living a hopeless life, because I hadn't ... taken God into account. I had simply ... given up."

His expression was still reflective as he continued. "But God apparently had another plan for me. Through you and Summer and the other children—and the penny whistle—He reminded me of something I already knew but had temporarily lost sight of. He reminded me that *hope is the music of the soul*. Without it, the human spirit cannot soar, cannot rise above the things of this earth ... and *sing*."

As Maggie watched, his gaze again went to the penny whistle in the cabinet on the wall. "I can't begin to explain how He did it. I'm not sure I understand *why* He did it. But I'm convinced that none of it was entirely for me, but was somehow meant for the entire town."

He turned back to Maggie. "There were changes after that," he said vaguely. "Subtle, gradual, most of them—but changes, all the same. In the town ... in the people ... and in me." Again he shook his head. "All I really know for certain, Maggie, is that on that night, God showed me that hope is, above all else, a gift—*His* gift. A gift that in reality has nothing at all to do with one's circumstances, but *everything* to do with His love. His love ... and our willingness to *trust* that love—that's what hope is. That's the music of the heart. The music of life."

The long, searching look he now turned on Maggie held a depth of fondness and affirmation that warmed her heart. "And if you will permit me to make an observation, Maggie, it would seem to me that in *your* life, He may well be composing an entire symphony."

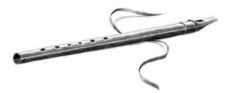

The End